To: Garrett
May God alwc

[handwritten inscription and signature]

death angel
A True Story

Michael J. Bishop

Writers Club Press
San Jose New York Lincoln Shanghai

Published by Writers Club Press
an imprint of iUniverse.com, Inc.

For information address:
iUniverse.com, Inc.
620 North 48th Street
Suite 201
Lincoln, NE 68504-3467
www.iuniverse.com

ISBN: 1-893652-89-0

Printed in the United States of America

PREFACE

When does the war end? The year is 1997, and it seems to me that it should have ended by now. Instead, I am sitting here staring at a lot of forms that the government would like me to complete, if I hope to be compensated for the debilitative effects of Post-Traumatic Stress Disorder (PTSD).

The material I have been given to read advises me that studies have confirmed that many Vietnam veterans have not readjusted successfully to civilian life. I'm not sure that I like the sound of that—possibly because it is the kind of statement that seems to be pointing a finger.

People who fail to adjust to the realities of life are often thought to be the source of their own problems, and occasionally, they are. Still, there are also those who have made a truly gargantuan effort to adjust to what would clearly be beyond anything that ordinary people, in ordinary times, would ever be expected to adjust to—and they did it, at least for the moment. The things is, they did not always understand the manner in which they accomplished this.

In my own case, I know that I have seen and heard and experienced some truly horrible things, but that I was also tuning them out, in much the same way that a person might tune out a radio station he wasn't really interested in.

Even so, my mind continued to register everything that was happening, cataloguing, labeling and filing away all the things I never really wanted to know or remember.

But then, at a reunion celebration, I suddenly ran into a wartime buddy who was dying of the effects of Agent Orange. He was sitting in a wheelchair and I saw what this process of dying had been doing to him.

Death had clearly come into the room with him, as it had with many others who were present that day, and it hovered about like a huge predatory bird. I could feel it creeping up slowly, determined to envelop what was left of these thin, frail bodies of my friends, and while I wanted to fight it off with all the strength that was in me, I sensed that the battle was already lost. The others knew it too. We had only to look at each other to know the truth.

There is a look in the eyes of a combat veteran that can only be understood by other combat veterans. They share a special brotherhood, forged out of the fires of hell that enables them to look at one another and think the words: "I know". And they do know! Anyone outside their circle would describe the look as sad, and sad is part of what it is, but only a part.

"This is what it's come to," my buddy in the wheelchair seemed to be saying. "This is what it was really all about."

Returning home from that reunion, everything I had ever managed to tune out about Vietnam was suddenly triggered. Here was a portion of the war that no one had ever told me about. It was like a cancer coming out of remission, attacking me with new strength, but now there was less of me to fight it.

Reliving so many horrific experiences in rapid succession soon took its mental and physical toll. I became deeply, even dangerously depressed. I found I could not deal with the depths of my own despair, nor could I seem to contrive any means of rising above it.

Just now, as I am writing this, I find myself fighting off yet another wave of anger, and hopelessness, and fear. It is a deadly combination—a truly immobilizing one. Unable to move off a certain spot, I find it is inertia rather that uncertainty or confusion that causes me to stay where I am.

There is no hint of any desire for change—nor is there even the desire to desire. I find myself thinking of my buddy in the wheelchair, a victim of Agent Orange. He and I are alike in certain ways. Death hovers over him, but there is also something hovering over me. It wants to claim something inside me that is still alive, whatever it is that still has the power to think, to decide, and to function.

This robotic person I am gradually becoming does not want me to feel guilt about surviving when others did not. It wards off the anxiety and nervousness, the depression and periodic flashbacks in the only way it knows how. It has been doing it all along, but there have been problems. Family members and friends do not understand my reasons for distancing myself, and I see the bewilderment and pain in their eyes. I am afraid that I will lose them if I do not talk about this, but I am also afraid that I might lose myself if I do.

I haven't wanted to look at those years again, but now, I suppose I will have to. The Vietnam Era Stress Inventory questionnaire I have been given to complete is asking me to address the fact that I have a service-connected disability, that it is treatable and also compensatable.

I have been told that it is possible to work through unpleasant memories and to stop having nightmares or other symptoms of Stress Disorder. I have been urged to learn more about myself through the therapy that is currently available, and to read some good books on the subject of PTSD.

In the midst of all this, it has suddenly occurred to me that reading a book might not be nearly as therapeutic as writing one.

I am not a writer. I am a Vietnam Vet. I cannot hope to express myself as a writer would, but maybe that is really for the best. Writers who bravely "take on a subject" may have talent, but they do not always have the voice. The truest voice can only come out of first-hand experience. I have that.

If my writing seems a bit too intense, too direct and unadorned, bear in mind that these are also true events I intend to describe.

I hope it will help others, along with myself, to relive it. The truth is, we never really *stopped* living it—even when we thought we did.

—Michael J. Bishop

Chapter 1

In the midst of a war, it would seem that the most prevalent thing in any soldier's mind is the thought of survival. At the outset, it probably is. But then something happens. The manner in which he continues to survive has a price that he never expected to pay. Although he knew he would be afraid, and outraged, and frustrated, and, of course, eternally thankful for every act of providence that somehow manages to spare him, there comes a day when he is faced with a somber and haunting truth.

More often than not, it comes in the form of a question. He awakens one morning, and because it is cold, he draws closer to the log he has been sleeping beside, in an effort to ward off the wind. But now, in the harsh light of day, he sees that the log is the body of a man, and that it is someone he knows. This comrade-in-arms he has come to rely upon, continues to help him in the only way he can, by providing his stiff and lifeless body as shelter.

Once war ceases to be whatever you imagined it to be, and becomes this endless game of Russian roulette, where people all around you moan and die—and there is no way to explain why it happens to them instead of you, something inside of you begins to crack. At first it is a hairline crack, barely noticeable, except for the fact that it has no business being there. It continues to widen over time, and although you do not know it, it is the beginning of an inner fragmentation.

Is there anyone on earth who isn't determined to make some sort of sense out of things? It is impossible to function with the idea that life itself is merely an accident, or a joke—and yet, in war, it would seem to be nothing more.

The person you were just talking and laughing with—the person whose vitality and spirit you most admired—lies suddenly dead at your feet. A moment earlier, only seconds before a sniper's bullet found him, he was the one you believed would make it through, if anyone ever would, but now he is gone, and you are still here.

The most painful question you will ever ask yourself begins to erode your inner confidence and certainty. Why is he dead? Why are you alive? And if you survive all this, what is the reason and the purpose?

Until I had stood with the dead and dying all around me, I felt no concern about such things. Throughout my life I had accumulated a different set of impressions about soldiers and soldiering, which began when I was barely three.

Because my father was a soldier, we lived on a military base in Fort Knox, Kentucky. Later we lived in Washington, and finally, we moved to Oklahoma.

By the time I was seven, I was going to the movies on Saturday afternoons, and one of the films I saw that most impressed me was *To Hell and Back* starring Audie Murphy. After seeing this movie, I was determined to become a soldier.

It was while we were living in a small town in Oklahoma that I joined the R.O.T.C. I remember how proud I was when I was first assigned to the color guard, where I guarded the American flag.

The following year I became a cadet officer, and in my senior year I was awarded a medal for being the best platoon leader.

At the time of my graduation, I was a cadet major in charge of a battalion. By then, my honesty and personal integrity had already been challenged by an Executive Officer who managed to acquire a copy of the final semester exam. Word spread quickly, and soon, every cadet officer had a copy of this test, and eventually, I did too.

I soon realized that I did not have the patience to memorize the answers to so many test questions, and I decided to wing it on my own.

What no one knew was that the Colonel administering the test had deliberately added a question that none of the others were prepared for. Those who answered by rote naturally missed this question, and once the results were all in, it turned out that I was the only one who had answered it correctly, and so, I was the only one who passed. As an A student, I received the highest academic average, while the others all failed because of their cheating.

Honor and duty had been firmly instilled in me by then, but there was also something else.

While still in school, I had been part of the A string on our football team, and my strategy as a lineman soon came to the coach's attention. He noticed that after I had tackled a man, I would pull his legs out, and then wait for him to get up so that I could inflict a little more pain in whatever way I could.

One day, the coach said, in front of the rest of the team, "Now this is the kind of football player we need! He's got a true killer instinct. What all of you need to remember is that you have to hit hard, harder than anyone else—and then make sure your opponent is down and dead."

Because no one had ever before described my character in such terms as these, I felt an immediate surge of pride. A person with true killer instincts was obviously admired for his courage and strength—and why not? Hadn't I once admired these same qualities in Audie Murphy?

It is interesting how insidiously the mind can be molded for battle. And then, of course, there are also inherent family traits of which a person is not necessarily aware. It was not until 1996 that I learned I was one quarter Indian. This, I realized, could easily account for certain wartime skills in which I appeared to excel. These included an uncanny talent for camouflage and concealment, the ability to read trails, and a method of sneaking up on the enemy that was similar to the stealth of a predatory animal.

And one thing more. During my college years, I had gotten into a fistfight with another student, and while such things were certainly known to happen, the outcome was a trifle unexpected. I ended up fracturing this kid's skull and crushing his rib cage, and afterwards, I was told that I had literally "pulverized" him. Although I hadn't intended to inflict any injuries of this magnitude, I was suddenly looking at a three-to-five year prison sentence.

Fortunately, because I was living in such a small town, residents were more inclined toward mediation than revenge. A local lawyer had little difficulty in convincing my parents, and the parents of the injured boy, that the best place for me was in the Army.

I was quick to agree since I wished, at all costs, to avoid going to prison. I enlisted at once, but was very nearly turned down because of my appalling driving record. It took a letter from the mayor and several members of the town council to get the Army to accept me. Once they had, I was sent on to Fort Polk, Louisiana.

Because I already knew a lot of the basics, including how to strip and clean a rifle, I was appointed platoon leader, and received an accelerated promotion to Private E-2 out of boot camp. Out of Advanced Individual Training (AIT), I became a PFC, but by then, I was experiencing some serious problems with my legs. Torn cartilage and ligaments were certainly no match for the Army's rigorous marching drills, and for a while, it appeared that I would be granted a medical discharge.

What kept this from happening had much to do with my own determination to stick things out, and eventually, I went to NCO Academy in Fort Beninng, Georgia.

While I was there, I was told the life expectancy of an NCO in Vietnam was approximately one week.

The NCO who came to address our class was a black man who had just returned from Vietnam. He placed particular emphasis on the fact that as NCO's, we would be responsible for the other people's lives, and that any bad decision we made could cause these people to die. "Think of living with that!" He said, and after class was over, I found I could think of nothing else. At the ripe old age of nineteen, I had begun to experience some highly conflicting emotions.At times, I felt truly invincible, and at other times, I was convinced that I was doomed.

After the NCO Academy, I went on to Ranger School, where I suffered another bout with my legs.

I returned to Fort Polk where I completed my OJT (On the Job Training), and from there, I was sent to Vietnam.

During this period, I decided to get married for reasons that were never entirely clear. I remember thinking that I might as well go ahead with it, and since my wife-to-be was a nice enough girl, it seemed like the right thing to do. In the back of my mind, I may have been thinking that this might be my only chance at married life, since Vietnam was a place I might never come back from.

In any case, I left the girl and went off to war, and since there had never been any time to construct a solid foundation under this marriage, her Dear John letter was only to be expected.

When I left for Vietnam on January 16, 1969, I had been assigned to the First Cavalry Division—Company D. Company D was called NO DEROS DELTA, DEROS being an abbreviation for Date of Estimated Return From Overseas.

My DEROS was a year after I got there, lacking one day. The Army set it up this way so that if they needed a man again, they could always say he had never actually spent a full one-year tour in Vietnam, and as long as this held true, he could always be called back in.

We went out into the jungle for a while, where we learned a number of things, including how to pack and unpack our rucksacks. This was a term for an infantryman's backpack, and I noticed that the men all seemed to have different ideas on what was important to take along, and what wasn't. One thing that was important was to repeatedly pack and unpack your rucksack without making even the slightest sound, and to learn how to do it in the dark, so that you could find things just by feel.

Over a period of one or two months, I learned what I needed to carry with me, and also, what I could afford to leave behind. One of the things I always carried was a machete, which I used to cut my way through the jungle. I also carried my Oklahoma flag, which made it a lot easier to attract other Oklahomans.

I had been in the jungle for a while before I became involved in my first firefight, or small arms battle. Not knowing what to expect, I tried to learn by modeling the actions of others. Still, a greenhorn is a greenhorn, however he may try to disguise it, and before very long, I learned that I had been classed among the FNG's (Fucking New Guys).

Our unit had its share of FNG's, and I was the sergeant. I had never been in charge of a squad or a team, and didn't even know how to take care of myself.

While I was still learning to do this, we received orders to move into an area with a lot of enemy activity, and a possible bunker complex. Ours was a Search and Destroy Mission. We were told we would be doing a helicopter combat assault on the area.

Because of the way I had been trained, and also because of what I had seen on television, I was expecting to see a nice clean rice field, but what I saw was a burned out area that had already been prepped, which simply meant that the artillery had all been fired, and holes and bomb craters had been dug to announce that we were coming. We arrived in a sortie, another term for a sudden and quick raid. Each sortie usually consisted of six soldiers to a chopper, with a four-man crew. Four sorties were capable of delivering 96 men, and in this case, I was in the third sortie—the third group of four. A combat assault, for any who are unfamiliar with this term, is a sudden rush or quick raid by helicopter.

Landing in the midst of this burned out field was like falling into a hot cauldron of burning ashes. Since we had no goggles to protect our eyes, it was difficult to see, and within minutes, we were filthy dirty, and stinking to high heaven.

Fortunately, it was not a hot landing zone—the enemy wasn't sitting there, waiting, This gave us time to establish a command center, and after that, it was patrol time.

Before very long the 3rd Platoon found a trail that had been well used, and this told us that the "gooks" had definitely been there. By now, we had learned that there were a number of ways of looking at a trail, and that each had its own story to tell.

A trail that was more than six inches wide, extending to perhaps three or four feet, was referred to as a highway or a "super trail". The manner in which the Vietnamese used their super trails was really quite ingenious. After reinforcing the frames of their bicycles, they could carry about five hundred pounds of rice in gunnysacks or woven bags, balanced on their bikes. The trail itself had to be wide enough for a man to stand beside the bike as he guided it down the trail.

Trails that were larger than this were called "major freeways". Such trails were often covered with bamboo, which the Vietnamese had woven together to give them a road that was free of mud.

We had already been warned that the bigger the trail, the more gooks we could expect to find in the area.

In this particular case, we had discovered a trail that was about a foot wide, close to a bunker complex or firebase, where the gooks were known to live.

After we had dropped off our heavy stuff, it was time to go out on patrol. We knew that the man who was left behind to guard the equipment would make good use of his time by digging a foxhole and filling sandbags while the rest of us were away.

As we started down the trail, moving closer to the bunker complex, we mentally prepared ourselves for some retaliation from the gooks. Each of the three platoons followed a separate trail.

When the point man in our platoon suddenly stopped, everybody else followed suit—not knowing exactly why—although we sensed that something was definitely wrong. For some reason, the Medic decided to go on ahead, and while I was examining an open area where some stakes had been driven into the ground, we heard a loud explosion. A few seconds later, Doc came running back bleeding from his left arm, and so, we quickly bandaged him up. My first thought was that I had triggered a booby trap, and that's when all hell broke loose.

At this point, we got our first taste of an AK-47, learning exactly what it sounded like. The AK-47 was a Communist made 7.62-caliber automatic assault rifle, a primary individual weapon used by enemy forces.

Falling to my knees proved to be a painful experience since I was carrying a 60-lb. rucksack at the time. Peering through the dense jungle, I could see the bushes moving, and I could hear the rounds, but I couldn't see who was doing the shooting.

Since this was the first time that any of us FNG's had been shot at, we all froze in our tracks, waiting for someone to give us permission to return fire. Finally, a more experienced sergeant yelled at us to get the hell out of there. At that point, I decided I had better start acting like a sergeant too, or possibly even John Wayne.

"Okay guys," I said, in what I hoped would pass for an authoritative tone of voice, "you'd better get out of here. I'll cover you."

Some of the younger FNG's were so scared that they just took off. By then, we had heard that a Cobra gunship had been sighted. This was a heavily armed helicopter used to support infantry troops, or to independently attack enemy units or positions. After the men had thought about it, they decided that this definitely meant trouble, and leaving a machine gun and a $6,000 Starlight scope behind, they took off running. The next time I looked around, I was the only one there.

I decided to keep hunting for whoever was doing the shooting. After this gook had fired a few more rounds at me, I heard other people shooting, and so, I did the same. As I fired in the direction that the rounds were coming from, the gook I couldn't yet see fired back. I fired again, and so did he, and after we had been doing this for a while, something told me to move. Crawling a few inches to the right, I barely missed being hit by four rounds that kicked up the dirt in the exact spot where I had been standing. Remembering the comment I'd heard about sergeants only lasting a week in Vietnam, it occurred to me that I had very nearly become part of that sobering statistic.

My next reaction was anger. I decided that I needed to go after whoever was shooting at me, that I needed to get really serious about this now, and that he and I would need to engage in our own little firefight.

Suddenly somebody shouted my name and ordered me to get out of there. I started to back up, firing the whole time, but then I tripped over a bush or a tree stump, and caught my heel on it, which caused me to fall flat on my back. Because I was still carrying my 60-lb. rucksack, I floundered around like some huge tortoise, before I finally managed to crawl out of there on my hands and knees.

Once we'd all managed to get back to a defensive position, somebody took a count. Then, when the Lieutenant learned that the FNG's had run off and left the Starlight scope and machine gun behind, he told us we would need to go after these things and that we were not to return until we had retrieved all of this gear. If the enemy got there first, we knew we would really be in trouble.

Sgt. Roy Weston, a close friend of mine, took his squad in ahead to set up security for us.

A few moments later, I saw the men carrying Weston back out and I saw that he'd been shot in the chest. After he was MediVaced back to the states, I remembered that he lived in Oklahoma, and decided that I would take the time to look him up after the war.

After the war! Who could possibly have known how long it would last, and how many would actually be lost.

In this, our initial firefight, we managed to kill one or two gooks before backing out. When we went back the next day, all the others were gone. We looked through the things they had left behind in an effort to determine where they might be headed, and once we had thoroughly examined everything, we blew the place up.

After Sgt. Weston left, I found that I missed my little conversations with him. From the very beginning, I had understood his strategy a little more clearly than the others, since it was similar to my own. At the end of each day, after we had gotten our night defensive position, I would find Weston and describe various things I had noticed throughout the day, and then I would ask him what it meant. Since he had been in Vietnam for quite a long while, he was a man worth listening to; he knew how to read every sign. I learned quite a bit from Weston, and felt a little like a fish out of water once he'd been shipped back to the states.

We had been instructed to move through the jungle in single file formation, keeping our eyes on the guy in front. If the advance man got hit, the odds were the rest of the line could survive, provided they got down fast enough. And as long as the advance man didn't get hit, he was up there cutting a trail for the rest of us, which made it a whole lot easier to get through.

Each day, a different squad of a platoon would walk point while the rest of us would follow along. There were times when I would find myself way at the end of the column, which I felt was the safest place to be, as long as the gooks weren't following behind.

The platoon that was walking point on any given day was also responsible for taking on any firefight that they might suddenly encounter. The other platoons remained in reserve, guarding the Forward Operating Base, unless an emergency call came in.

Each night we cut down small trees with our machetes, which wasn't a whole lot of fun, but it did build strong bodies. We got to know one another a whole lot better while we were doing things like that. And seeing how the others operated told us a lot about how they thought, and how well they could be counted on in an emergency.

Because I was a sergeant and a squad leader, it wasn't long before I was told that I would need to take out my first ambush. A platoon sergeant by the name of Woody Hanks assigned a group of men to me, introducing them as my fire team.

During a quick meeting with my company commander, a spot on a map was pointed out, and I was told that this was where we would be setting up our ambush. The site turned out to be about one grid square away—one grid square measuring one thousand meters by one thousand meters.

Once I had everything lined up, I got my squad together and then had a little talk with my point man, whose name was Artie Atwood. I explained to Artie that we were going out 1,200 meters, across an open valley, and that we would be setting up an ambush just inside the woodline.

Artie looked at me and said, "Fuck you, dude. I ain't going over there. Five or six of us that far from the rest of the company would be suicide." At that point, he reminded me that he was a short-timer, with less than sixty days to serve.

Although his belligerence took me by surprise, I could tell that he was serious. Deciding to lead by example, I said, "Tell you what, Artie—I'll walk point," which may or may not have convinced him, and also the others, that I wasn't about to send my men where I wasn't willing to go myself.

After we'd had our little meeting, everyone looked at me in disbelief. Finally, somebody said, "Sarge, I don't know what you mighta learned in the NCO Academy, but over here, we don't do that kind of shit."

I responded to this by reminding them that I was a sergeant in the United States Army, and that I had no intention of disobeying an order.

"I'm going!" I told them emphatically. "And you're going with me." After that I, threatened to court-martial every one of them, and that seemed to get their attention.

When somebody finally asked what time we were saddling up, I knew I had enlisted their cooperation. We gathered up all our combat gear, including our claymore mines, which were command-detonated, anti-personnel mines. Everything within fifty feet of the front of a claymore instantly stopped breathing as they were designed to saturate an area of sixty degrees across the front, with 750 steel ball bearings.

Once we had started out, with me walking point, I never looked back. Along the way I noticed some things I didn't like, and cautiously dropped to one knee. I kept watching the woods as I waved for the others to come on ahead. When nobody showed up, I waved again, still keeping my eyes trained on the woods. When I finally turned and looked back, I saw that my men were about 200 meters behind me. This time, I waved at them with angry impatience, but all they did was flip me off.

Walking back to where they were, I said, "What the hell is going on?"

A spokesperson for the group advised me that I could do whatever I liked, but that they had no intention of following along. "Once you're not so new," he said, "you'll start to see things differently." At this point I was beginning to feel that these guys had decided I was going to die first if I decided to push the issue.

"Okay," I said, with a grin, "so where do you want to set up?"

Once they had picked the place, we set up our ambush about 150 feet in front of the bunker with some of our guys in it. We warned the men in the bunker about the location of our ambush so that they wouldn't accidentally blow their claymores, which were capable of killing us instead of the gooks.

The lesson I learned from all this was that if somebody told you to go a distance of 2,000 meters, your best bet was to tell them to go themselves. This was the way they did things in a line company.

We were constantly getting intelligence reports, and one of them informed us that they had discovered a major bunker complex in the province on Tay Ninh. Usually, a major bunker complex is so well hidden and so well camouflaged that it is impossible to see it from the air. For that matter, it can also be hard to see on the ground.

This particular complex covered six grid squares, which meant that it was 2,000 meters, or a mile wide, and a mile-and-a-half deep. It contained, among other things, an underground hospital, which was truly amazing since the entire project had been dug out by hand. Over a period of time, the enemy had literally honeycombed the Iron Triangle with a sophisticated complex of tunnels, and these underground networks provided them with facilities for aid stations, training rooms, supply depots, and even some administrative offices.

The discovery of this major complex meant that we had found ourselves a whole lot of gooks, and the plan was to surround them after the B-52 strike and to take prisoners in order to gain information.

Our battalion of one thousand men flew in and started hitting them with everything we had. After the place had been arclighted (another term for a B-52 bombing mission), it was discovered that it hadn't been a good hit, that only a corner of the complex had actually been damaged.

After making a quick sweep of the place, we decided that the gooks were already gone since the bunker appeared to be empty. Or so we thought.

While I was standing off to one side, smoking a cigarette, a guy named Quincy opened up on the bunker just in front of us. We had noticed the bunker, but none of us had gotten around to looking inside. When Quincy saw the gook, who had his sights on me, he started shooting, and when he did, the gook dropped down and crawled inside the bunker.

Knowing he was in there, we called the chieu hoi, (this is an enemy soldier who has rallied to the South Vietnamese government). After the chieu hoi had been given an opportunity to talk in Vietnamese to the gook inside the bunker, urging him to throw out his weapon and give himself up, we realized that we had a real die-hard on our hands.

At this point, Artie Atwood and I did a belly-crawl toward the bunker and threw a fragmentation grenade inside. Since the frags only had a four-second delay, we scrambled to get out of there as quickly as we could,

"You figure we got him?" Artie asked, after the frag had exploded.

"Beats me," I said.

Somebody suggested that we throw three more frags into the bunker, which I did. I tossed them into a hole that measured about 6 x 6, and once they had all exploded, it was unanimously decided that I should be the one to go in. Since I was the sergeant, I was once again being called upon to lead by example, or so it seemed.

Meanwhile, we saw some green tracers, a kind of ammunition the gooks were using that contained a chemical compound to mark the flight of their projectiles by leaving a trail of smoke or fire. We realized then that another gook was trying to cover the one we were after.

We decided to lay low for a while, but our objective was still to get to the gook inside the bunker. Because it was a Z-type bunker, we knew we might never get to him if he was holed up at the other end.

In a 6 x 6 bunker, it's pretty easy to see the other opening, and once we'd found another door, we decided to throw some frags in there. At this point, Atwood crawled up with his rifle, waiting for the other gook to start shooting.

With only a grenade in my hand that I'd already pulled the pin on, I crawled on top of the bunker and looked into the opening. Suddenly I saw the gook standing just inside the opening, holding an AK-47 rifle. I was only about three feet away from him, and Atwood was approximately the same distance away, but kneeling off to the right, where he couldn't see what I could see. I realized that if the gook turned ever so slightly, he would be able to see Atwood and that he could kill him in an instant. This scared me so badly that I jumped off the bunker and started running towards our guys. Looking back to see if Atwood had spotted the gook, I failed to see a thick growth of bamboo directly in front of me. Hitting those hard, woody stems that can reach a height of twenty or thirty feet, I felt as if I had run into a brick wall. Even as I fell, I still had a death grip on the grenade, and once I'd regained my feet, I ran back to the bunker, certain that Atwood was going to die.

As I threw the grenade at the gook inside the bunker, I yelled at Atwood to get out of the way. When the gook fired the AK-47, I was holding my hand outstretched, with the fingers spread apart, and the shots actually flew through the spaces between my fingers. There are so many dramatic life-and-death thoughts that a person can have at such moments, but the only thing I thought of was an incident that had occurred one Fourth of July when I was a child, when, I lit a firecracker and then forgot to throw it.

Chapter 2

Coming that close to being shot was an experience that could only be felt in retrospect. In the instant it happened, I felt nothing. But a few minutes later, I suddenly felt everything. I was shaking uncontrollably as the adrenaline surged through my body. For the first time, I felt myself experiencing fear after-the-fact, and it was not only powerful, but also immobilizing.

I heard the company commander yell, "What the hell's the matter with you, soldier? You gonna kill that sucker or not?" As if from a great distance, I heard the lieutenant's response to this. "I think we got him, sir. All we have to do is get him out of there."

What I was thinking as I heard this little exchange was something on the order of: "Why don't you bring your butt up here and see how brave you are, sucker!" Which pretty much summed up my feelings toward the company commander.

As everyone looked in my direction, I moved forward and prepared to crawl in. The hole in the bunker was so small that I couldn't go in with an M-16 rifle, so they gave me a .45 automatic pistol. The problem was, it hadn't been out of its holster for such a long time that it had frozen up. It took a while to get it to work.

As I cautiously entered the hole, I could see a man's leg, and since it wasn't moving, I figured this gook was probably dead, or else, mortally wounded. Still, there were other things to worry about. Since this was a major bunker complex, I knew that this small space might only be the entrance to something much larger—an entire hospital, perhaps, or even administrative offices, where a number of others could be waiting.

The thought of what might actually be in there caused my heart to pound erratically. When I finally crawled inside, I saw that the leg I had been looking at earlier was no longer attached to the man it had once belonged to. He was sitting propped up against a wall, staring at his own leg, but then, when I looked more closely, I saw that his eyes were glazed and unmoving, and I realized that this was to be my first confirmed kill.

I had done it. I had killed someone. I thought of *To Hell and Back* with Audie Murphy, and tried to remember the reason for my fascination with that film. It had all seemed so different up there on the screen. There had been something heroic and dangerously exciting about it all. There hadn't been any question about Audie's mission, about its purpose and importance. But now I was looking at a dead man, someone I did not know, had never known, and yet there was a history to this person. Someone he knew and loved would care about this, and grieve deeply; many lives would probably be disrupted because of what had happened here today. And one of those lives, I knew, would have to be mine.

Only a few moments earlier, I had not yet done this. Already I mourned the loss of that person, the one with no blood on his hands, the one I could never go back to.

Once I'd pulled him out, everyone crowded around and made the usual comments. "Yep, you got him all right." " He's deader'n hell, no question about it." "Nice going, Sarge."

I felt weak and sick inside, and also angry and disgusted to think that I had killed a man, that I had had to kill this man, and that I would probably have to kill more. What made it even worse was that I seemed to have earned a new kind of respect from these men, and several even took the time to pat me on the shoulder and comment on my courage. Courage! Even now, my heart was still pounding so fiercely that I could hardly hear what anyone was saying.

I watched as someone closed the dead man's eyes and then rummaged through his pockets, looking for anything of value, including such souvenirs as an NVA belt buckle with a star on it, which we all knew would be worth its weight in gold back in the States. At one point, I actually had four of them, but ended up giving them all away.

By the time we had covered the body, our hands were all coated with blood. In order to clean myself up, I had to use my two quarts of water and after that, I nearly died of thirst.

The men had been talking amongst themselves, and suddenly, I realized they were talking about me. When they finally volunteered a few of their personal opinions, I discovered that they didn't think I would last very long out there because of everything that had already happened to me. In the first thirty days, I had already experienced two life-threatening situations, and appeared—at least in their eyes—to be targeted for an early demise.

At one and the same time, I was considered to be the most valiant member among us, the man who could always be counted on to get the job done. Looking back on it, I think it was more a case of being too stupid to be scared, and having been programmed to do certain things certain ways, I simply went ahead and did them.

This was the beginning of my psychic realignment, something every soldier must go through in order to continue on with the unimaginable reality of killing in order to avoid being killed. This profound transformation was necessary so that I could do what I had come to Vietnam to do. Although I was beginning to feel like a stranger to myself, I thought this was good. The person I didn't know was certainly easier to deal with than the one I did know. I didn't need a voice inside my head that was constantly criticizing— one that seemed intent upon making me feel guilty and ashamed.

Two days later, when we found ourselves engaged in some more firefights with other bunker complexes, I suddenly heard somebody call my name. Dropping my gear, I crawled over to the lieutenant, who said, "We've got a man down."

By now, everyone was yelling, "Andy's up there. He's been hit! Somebody go get him!"

Although our platoon had pretty well surrounded the area, no one volunteered to go after Andy Fletcher, a black man, whose original intention was to fire an M-79 grenade launcher into the bunker. Although the launcher was designed to be fired from a distance of 15 or 20 feet. Andy had gotten within six feet of his target. When a gook saw what he was about to do, he shot him. The bullet entered through Andy's neck, and came out his back, just under his shoulder blade. By the time I reached him, he was bleeding profusely from both holes. I got everybody in place, and they laid down a base of fire while I crawled about 20 feet and quickly pulled him back. After that, Atwood and I carried him to a MediVac, and loaded him on board. He was basically unconscious at the time, due to loss of blood, and later he died of his injuries.

We bombed the devil out of that place, and afterwards, discovered a major cache of ammunition and explosives. It was indeed fortunate that we didn't manage to hit it, since if we had, the explosion would have blown us all to bits.

By the time we got into our next firefight, I had already made some friends, which was something we had all been warned not to do. Still, I had gotten to know this guy named Lonnie Davis, and after a while, Lonnie, became my buddy.

Now that I was no longer considered an FNG, I had a squad that seemed willing to back me up, and Lonnie became my machine gunner. He was pretty solid and down-to-earth, considering that he'd had a rather privileged background. As a civilian, he had held down a high-paying job, owned a Corvette, and lived pretty high on the hog. But after I'd managed to save his life a few times, and covered his ass a few other times, Lonnie became my main man.

Another guy I got pretty close to was Sgt. Henry Akins, who was on leave when I first came into the unit. Once I really had a chance to get to know him, I knew I had nothing to fear as long as Akins was around. He had earned a couple silver stars, and was on his third tour of Vietnam, and whatever Sgt. Akins said, was pretty much the way it was.

We began another Combat Assault by setting up a fixed operation base (FOB) and then, went back out, looking for trouble. This time we were following a super trail wide enough to accommodate a two-and-a-half ton truck. Having hit this major supply line, we knew we had better get ready.

There was a bunker complex, of course, and that afternoon, one of our men killed a gook, a point man. After that, part of our unit went off patrol with Sgt. Akins, while the other half stayed behind to secure the FOB and dig in. Since I was in the group that stayed behind, I was busily digging foxholes and cutting fields of fire when suddenly, all hell broke loose.

Soon after the firefight had started, the lieutenant called me over to say that Lonnie Davis's machine gun had jammed. This never happened unless the man with the gun didn't know how to use it, or else, had failed to clean it properly.

Anyway, when he tried to shoot some gooks, the gun jammed, and no one was killed. Because everyone was obviously outraged at this, I quickly assured them that the gun would be checked out, and that nothing like this would ever happen again. Once Lonnie and I had personally cleaned the gun, we dry-fired it, and it worked perfectly.

The same night, we sent out a squad to set up an ambush on that super trail and killed ourselves a few more gooks. The next morning, we checked out our dead, and then headed for the bunker complex. The killing business was really good.

Two of our mortar men were named Charlie Grissom and Pete Sturgis. Charlie was a cowardly sort who liked to remind me whenever he had the chance that he was a mortar man who really belonged on the firebase. He also preferred to walk behind me rather than in front.

After we had finished digging our foxholes and cutting our fields of fire, we rallied with the rest of the troops, reorganized, and headed back to the bunker complex for an afternoon attack.

When the enemy started attacking us with some mortar of their own, a lot of our guys jumped into some bomb craters that were about 20 feet deep and 20 feet wide. For the moment, it seemed like the best line of defense so I decided to do the same. No sooner had I jumped into a bomb crater than another guy jumped in on top of me, and the next thing I knew, he was walking all over my rifle. I started to cuss him out but then I saw that he was all shot up, and stumbling around in a daze. Although he'd been right next to me, I never even saw him get hit. By then, I was back out of the bunker, trying to figure out what was going on.

Meanwhile, another guy who was standing about three feet away, suddenly grabbed his rifle, held it up over his head and started firing aimlessly. In the process, he very nearly shot me in the foot, so I yelled at him, and this seemed to bring him to his senses. I could see how terrified he was, and lowered my voice a little as I urged him to look where he was shooting so that he wouldn't end up hitting his own people.

The next time we tried the machine gun, it jammed again and although we didn't know why, we didn't have time to think.

At this point, I felt I couldn't stay by the bomb crater any longer. After all, I was the man in charge of the sector. Everybody was shooting, mostly in the same direction, but I wasn't always sure what they were shooting at. As I looked at these guys, I could see that they were in a state of near panic. Some were so terrified that I think they would have taken off, if they had only known which way to go. As it was, they felt they had no choice but to stay together and fight.

The next thing that happened was that we got an emergency call from our FOB. We learned that while we were hitting the gooks from one side, they were circling around us, coming in from behind, going through, and cutting our unit in half. We were told we were needed back at the FOB to help keep the enemy from taking over our bunkers and supplies, and ambushing us when we came back.

Once we had managed to sabotage this plan, we had ourselves a little snack and then went back out again.

While Lonnie was getting his butt chewed out a second time over his jammed machine gun, another guy named Barry Phipps pulled out his little New Testament Bible and started reading it. Barry was a grenadier, an M-79 grenade launcher.

Once the fight started up again, we gave them everything we had, and after a while Sgt. Akins started back up the trail. He was dressed in Ho Chi Minh slicks, gook shoes, a pith helmet, and vest, and was carrying an AK-47. He looked just like a gook.

Anytime there was a firefight, you could always count on Akins to run to the front, and take right after those gooks. He was kill-crazy and damned proud of it.

On this particular day, I called out "Hey, Sarge, they're over here." After a few minutes, I called to him again. Suddenly, all the fighting stopped and that was when Akins started walking up the trail. The next thing we heard were four shots, four solid shots perfectly placed so that Akins' body was laced from the right to the left. He dropped to his knees and then just sort of lay back, with his AK-47 lying across his body.

As I continued to call for Akins, I heard Pete Sturgis say, "Forget it, man. He's dead."

A cloud of silence seemed to fall over the entire jungle as I looked at Pete and thought about what he'd just said. It couldn't be true, I thought, because nobody ever killed Akins. He seemed unstoppable, and yet he hadn't been. I wanted to call out to him again, louder this time, loud enough to arouse him from that deep and final sleep, and bring him back to us, where he belonged.

Akins dead! The thought of it could be felt like a blow to the stomach, and for a moment, I think I may even have doubled up in pain. I thought of his two silver stars, and his three tours of duty which hadn't provided him with any sort of life insurance at all. The cold reality of it was truly overwhelming, and it took me a while to recover.

At the end of that day we had wounded lying all over the place, but because the enemy was still flanking us, we knew it would be hard to get them out.

Suddenly we heard an agonizing scream. It turned out to be Barry Phipps, who had crawled up the trail with his M-79 grenade launcher to either help Sgt. Akins himself, or to protect anyone who might try to pull him out. Barry Phipps, with his little New Testament Bible, had been determined to do what he could, and all that was necessary, to assist and support whoever might need him.

Lonnie Davis was sitting there with us when the company commander gave the order to pull out. At that point, I told Lonnie to lay down a base of fire while we were pulling our wounded back to keep the enemy from following us. Lonnie fired into the bushes where Phipps was hiding, and not just once, but several times, hitting him in the buttock and pelvic areas. Later, when I checked Phipps out, I saw the extent of his injuries. His wound was so large that one 3 x 5 dressing wouldn't even cover the hole. The machine gun fire had caught him in the left pelvic area, and exited through the left cheek of his buttock.

While we did what we could for Phipps, Davis started crying and screaming, "I've shot one of my own men. God forgive me!" He kept carrying on like that until I finally grabbed him and shook him really hard.

"We don't have time for any of this shit!" I yelled. "We need to get the fuck out of here!"

This seemed to bring Lonnie to his senses and he grabbed up his machine gun and what was left of the ammo, while I carried Phipps, and somebody grabbed up his pack.

Once we'd gotten Phipps back to FOB, we started cutting down trees to give the chopper a place to land.

Davis was still pretty hysterical, and it was the wrong time for the lieutenant to get on his case, but he did anyway. Afterwards, I sat Davis down and talked to him quietly, reminding him that things like this sometimes happened in the middle of a war, and that everyone knew it had been an accident.

Lonnie's answer to this was, "I'm not carrying that machine gun anymore, I don't care if they court martial me, or even kill me! I'm just not carrying it!"

I tried to reason with him, insisting that we needed a machine gun.

"Then let somebody else do it!" he argued. "The fact that Phipps is still alive is just a fluke, if you want to know the truth."

I asked him what he meant by that.

"The gun jammed again," he told me. "If it hadn't. I'd have kept right on firing, and Barry Phipps would be dead."

Once he had told me this, I made a point of putting that machine gun on the next supply bird that came in, switching it out for a replacement.

Meanwhile, the lieutenant, who hadn't finished harassing Lonnie Davis, threw Phipps' grenade launcher at him, and said "Here! See if you can work this piece of shit!"

Davis could not fail to notice, even as the rest of us did, that the grenade launcher was covered with Phipps' blood.

Pulling Davis aside, I helped him to clean up the launcher, in much the same way that we had cleaned up the machine gun. We worked silently, since neither of us knew if we could control our emotions. Just then, I was raging inside over the way the lieutenant had chosen to handle the situation. I tried not to think about all the ways in which I wanted to retaliate. I had heard stories about lieutenants and other officers being killed by their own men, and I was beginning to understand the reasons why.

Throughout the entire war, we ran on a mixture of anger and fear, and out of this came moments of incredible frustration. The screaming inside my head was often so loud that I felt sure that the enemy would hear it. There were times when every cell and tissue in my body seemed to vibrate with supercharged adrenaline, and I felt ready to strike out and do anything. All this pent-up anger had nowhere to go, until the next firefight with Charlie. It was this that drove the American soldier to become the toughest and meanest of all military men, along with the endless frustration of not knowing why the hell he was even there, or why he was doing what he was doing.

From what we had been told, it had something to do with the "domino theory" which began when President Eisenhower wrote a letter to the President of South Vietnam, in which he promised more American support for that country. Eisenhower maintained that South Vietnam was like a domino among other dominoes, (or nations), in that if one of them fell to the Communists, then the rest of the democratic nations of Southeast Asia would inevitably fall as well.

Americans who were in Vietnam during the idealism of the mid -1960s believed they were fighting Communism in Vietnam to prevent the domino effect from encroaching upon American shores. But as the war went on and on, the struggle to free the South Vietnamese people from Communist domination lost the support of the American people back home who erroneously perceived it to be a civil war between the North and the South Vietnamese. After a while, American soldiers and civilians alike became confused as to whether the war had anything to do with either communism or democracy. And so, it became a nucleus for civil unrest on American shores, and a burdensome cross to bear for the veterans who finally returned.

But while we were there, we thought that what we were facing right then was the worst of it. PTSD meant nothing at this point. I doubt that very many of us had even heard of it.

Once we had made it back to our FOB, we called for a Cobra gunship to come in and pound these suckers, and put them back in their place and give us some time to get out. This heavily armed helicopter was used to support infantry troops, when it wasn't independently attacking enemy units or positions.

Although our Forward Observer called in the proper location of the enemy bunker, the Cobra's gunner apparently believed that some mistake had been made. After making some hasty calculations of his own, he came up with a new target site, and instead of firing on the bunker complex, he ended up firing on us.

The end result was that a number of our men were seriously wounded, and once they were MediVaced out, we were seventeen people short in our platoon.

The next morning, after very little sleep, and while we were trying to recover from all this, we once again prepared ourselves for a nighttime hit, which was the gooks' favorite time to attack. By now, we had come to realize that we had bitten off far more than we could chew. We were a company size unit of about 100 men, taking on what seemed to be a thousand enemy soldiers. They were everywhere! When we would try to flank them, they were there, meeting our flank with soldiers trying to flank us. The results were always the same. It was a chess game with each player using up all their pawns in an effort to protect the King and Queen.

Much to our surprise, they did not launch the attack we were expecting, and the next morning, we set up some ambushes.

Since the third platoon had gotten hit so hard, they came to us and one of them asked me for a grenadier. The only one I had was Lonnie, who was still shaken over the Barry Phipps incident, and I knew it would be an extremely bad move to send him out. Still, our lieutenant, in his infinite wisdom, saw fit to send Lonnie out, primarily because he was still venting over the machine gun incident. As a consequence, soon after cleaning the blood off Phipps' gun, Lonnie went off with a new squad and a new squad leader whom he had never worked with before.

The place where they decided to set up an ambush had already been selected by the gooks for the very same purpose. As a result, there wasn't time for anybody to ambush anybody. Having accidentally run into each other, they had themselves a little firefight, right then and there.

The day I sent Lonnie Davis out with the third platoon was also the last day I ever saw him. He got shot in the head and when the radio brought us this news, we felt certain we knew what it meant. But Lonnie had a strong will to live, and when the medic examined him, he said, "No, wait a minute, get him a Medivac—he's still alive."

Once they brought Lonnie in on a stretcher, one of the mortar men, Charlie Grissom, tried to load him into the chopper. But because he was so cowardly and scared, he dropped the stretcher, causing Lonnie to hit his head on the skid, and that is what finally killed him.

Here was another first, as I would later come to think of it. The loss of my first "best friend in Vietnam" was a moment that was destined to remain with me, not only throughout the war, but also for all the days that followed. I thought of the warnings we had all been given, the warnings against forming any close attachments. How was this possible? I wondered. Knowing we might never see our loved ones again made it necessary, even vital, to fabricate a family of sorts in this strange and alien land. Man was not designed for a solitary life. It was senseless to expect us to suddenly adopt that manner of existence, particularly when we were forced to rely upon one another for survival. How was it possible to make such demands, and then turn away coldly from the very ones who had covered our backs? No, it wasn't possible. Lonnie Davis had been my friend, my foxhole buddy, my confidant, my brother and my pal. And now he was dead, and because a freak accident had been involved, I was enraged—enraged at the war, and Charlie Grissom, and the stupidity of all that we had gotten ourselves involved in. But there wasn't any time for emotional displays, or even a moment to sort it all out. There wasn't even time for a funeral service.

But once we got back to the firebase, I made a point of going to ordinance and sure enough, the machine gun Lonnie had been struggling with had a bad ejector. The times it failed to fire hadn't been Lonnie's fault at all. For some reason, it seemed suddenly important to make this abundantly clear. I immediately advised the lieutenant who had always been so hard on Lonnie and, after that, I continued to look for ways to vindicate my friend, doing this now in his memory.

Chapter 3

We fought for six days, six bloody days of basically useless combat since we never really accomplished anything. At the end of the sixth day, the length of our casualty list made it obvious that a B-52 bombing mission, otherwise known as arc-lighting, would have been a far better solution.

Witnessing all those mangled bodies, torn to shreds by bullets, grenades, and heavy artillery, affected me deeply. I would never forget what I was looking at. Waves of grief, sorrow, pain, fear and anger suddenly converged into a single emotion that had no name, but after all that, it became the fuel that I ran on. The body count was our way of keeping score. Whoever killed the most was "da winner".

And grotesque statistics known as a "body count" were the enemy's measurement of victory—just as they were ours. When people died, somebody was winning. Winning what? And for what? That was the real question.

I had begun to have a sense of futility about things. It is a bad feeling, extremely counter-productive to what a soldier has taken upon himself to do. Still, senseless battles and senseless killing are hard to call by any other name. The military strategy was truly laughable at times, and the stupid blunders that caused the untimely death of such fine young men as Lonnie Davis were hard to swallow.

The rage I managed to repress at that time would return to haunt me in later years. When it began to surface in strange and inappropriate ways, it laid the foundation for many failed relationships and an overall maladjustment to society, perhaps because it was impossible for me to understand peace as others understood it. Inside myself, there was no peace, only grim memories of the kind of violence and brutality that is destined to play itself out over a lifetime.

After our six long days of futile fighting, a MediVac chopper arrived to extract the wounded and dead. It came without weapons of any kind, which they weren't allowed to carry, and left behind all the gear that belonged to the soldiers they loaded on board. After that, it was up to us to haul off everything we didn't want the gooks to have, and since there was so much of it, we threw it all into a pile—everything except the rifles and ammunition, and set it all afire. Although we could certainly have used the extra rations, we simply couldn't carry it all—and not wanting to leave it for the enemy, we burned it with everything else.

In the days that followed Lonnie's death, I often thought about my conversations with him, which included some thoughts about the future.

He told me about a couple service stations he owned back home, including one that was strategically placed along a main four-lane highway.

"Once we get out of this," he said, "you can come and work for me. And I'm not just talking about a job either. If you'll run my stations for me while I set up a few more, you'll make more money than you've ever seen in your life."

In the jungles of Vietnam, Lonnie Davis thought of me as his only friend, and perhaps it was actually true.

Once we got back to the firebase, we all got stinking drunk, which helped us get through the memorial services for all of the men we had lost.

One thing I noticed was that I immediately became less functional when anger was not a part of whatever I was doing. The military had trained us to emphasize anger, and to downplay everything else. Anger was fuel and courage, and even a philosophy of life, and that was how we managed to get from one day to the next.

After the bombing mission, we were sent back into the same area to conduct another combat assault. This was quite an experience since, of course, we were accustomed to walking on solid ground, but now this ground was suddenly powder. I could feel myself sinking in up to my ankles, as I cautiously moved along, through heavy clouds of fog and dust. What few trees were still left standing, were dead and broken, and as I passed beneath them, I felt crumbling particles of tree bark and singed leaves falling down around my shoulders. Before very long, we were all liberally covered with dust and soot, and our faces looked as if we were wearing masks.

Once we'd gone back into the bunker complex, we found paraphernalia belonging to the Vietnamese, but we never found a single body. After we'd blown up the bunker, we looked around a bit, but even though our sensors were going off, which usually meant that some gooks were around, there was nothing to be seen.

Soon afterwards, we were transferred to another area that had already been prepped. They'd shot all the artillery and everything seemed to be on fire, which is all we needed on a one hundred degree day.

Once we'd established our firebase, we sent our patrols out, and while I was listening to the radio, I heard somebody say: "Man, we found ourselves a super trail, a powder trail, and more damned gooks than you could ever imagine." A little while after that, somebody found a wire, or land line, which worked just like a telephone wire for purposes of communication. We managed to bug the line and then listened as the gooks sent messages back and forth, which verified that there were a lot of them in the area.

By mid-afternoon, we'd already gotten ourselves involved in a few little skirmishes, the kind of thing where the gooks try to hit-and-run, and then get us to follow them so that they could spread us out.

Although we could hear people running in every direction, we never saw a soul. Judging by the noise, we figured we were up against more gooks here than we could comfortably deal with. We had positioned ourselves at the edge of an open area, which is usually the best place to be, because the enemy wasn't apt to run through an open area in order to attack us.

The first gooks we saw were about five hundred yards away, and while some of our men started shooting, it was a waste of ammo at that great a distance. It took a while for our battalion commander to decide that there was more here than we could handle, but the decision was finally made to arc-light the area.

We pulled out early that evening, then went back to the firebase where we settled ourselves down for a good hot meal. After that, we sort of kicked back and took the rest of the night off, a rare experience in the jungles of Vietnam.

I remember that somebody pulled out a calendar and tried to figure out what day it was. As if this really mattered.

By this time, I'd lost all of my earlier impressions of war, those that I'd formed as a youngster when I was watching Audie Murphy on the big silver screen. Whatever I'd once thought war was about had precious little to do with the grim reality of it. Watching your friends die, listening to their screams, and living in the midst of total devastation was a far cry from the nonsensical heroics that Hollywood had somehow created for an impressionable young boy to admire. Admire! God, there was nothing to admire here. What it finally came down to was doing what you could, when you could, and then, just moving on.

I was frequently frightened out of my wits, afraid I wouldn't make it through the day, the hour, or even the next few minutes. And one thing I learned, along with everyone else, was that ordering an arc-light wasn't exactly like ordering a pizza. You had to wait your turn, and a lot of things could happen in the interim.

Whenever we encountered some gooks and started giving them a little flak, I had a sense of stirring up a hornet's nest, since the situation was very similar. In the case of hornets, even if you managed to wipe out the major portion, you can be sure that the ones who are left are going to be pretty damned mad. And the same held true for these gooks.

As time went on, we all became extremely superstitious about quiet. A little of it was okay, but when it began to drag on, when things became eerily silent, and remained that way for what seemed like a very long time, we were instantly on edge. Not surprisingly, this kind of quiet was often the forerunner of a sudden ambush. With no time to get ourselves prepared, we could find ourselves in the midst of a mad scramble to survive.

Even on the best days, fighting in Vietnam was a strange experience. A firefight, as far as I could tell, was nothing more than a sudden barrage of gunfire, which would eventually stop, without anyone having actually called a 'Cease Fire', and then, after a brief pause, things would start up again. While I was trying to figure out what the rules of the game were, it suddenly occurred to me that there were no rules. As we continued traipsing through the jungle, we acted more or less instinctively; there was no real military strategy involved. We simply carried the ball for as long as we could, or until we fumbled it, and then it was somebody else's turn.

The next firebase we were transported to was close to a rubber plantation where some Mama-sans was selling some beer. After pooling our funds, we invested in some six-packs of gook beer, which had a lot of impurities in it, and smelled a lot like embalming fluid, but it was better than nothing at all.

We had been told that we would be going out with another unit, and when the time came, we took part in another combat assault, which was relatively uneventful.

Once we had teamed up with Bravo Company, there were two hundred of us, which made me feel a whole lot better about things.

We decided to set up our firebase at a point where two trails came together, so that anyone who came down that trail would be forced to encounter us. We were in the midst of setting up our night defensive positions, when I was told that it was our turn to make a patrol. The exact instructions were to cloverleaf in front of our area, a couple hundred meters ahead, and check out the AO (Area of Operations).

Taking the whole squad with me, I walked point, and after about a hundred meters, we noticed some bunker that were only partially dug, with no tops on them, and no camouflage. The next thing I noticed was a trail leading to another bunker with piles of fresh dirt surrounding it. At this point, everyone else sort of fell back as they waited for me to go ahead and check the area out. I was about 30 or 40 feet away from this bunker when I got the eeriest feeling. I was standing close to a tree, and as I continued to look at the bunker and the trail in front of me, I pulled my head back, and that's when I heard a loud explosion. The tree shattered like glass, and in that same instant, I knew I'd been hit. The force of whatever had hit me knocked me to the ground, and I lay there, with my head pointing toward our defensive side, with my rifle pointing toward my feet. My troops immediately hit the ground, and lay there, looking around, trying to determine where the explosion had come from.

I began to move ever so slightly, and then I heard someone call out, "Sarge, are you all right?"

Before I could answer, everything happened at once. Rounds of ammunition began flying over my head, only inches away. I looked toward my men, who hadn't yet begun to return fire; they were still hugging the ground, trying to spare themselves.

Because I was literally paralyzed with fear, it was easy to lie there as if I was dead, and this probably worked in my favor. I was lying face down, with my rear end in the air, and then, as the same voice asked again, "Sarge, are you all right?" Several more rounds of fire went flying by. By this time, my teeth were so tightly clenched that I felt they were going to break off. By now, I had begun second-guessing the enemy's strategy. If they could wound me bad enough to get me to scream, some of my men might run out and try to pull me out of the line of fire, and that's when they'd get us all.

After a minute or two, I heard someone else call out, but in a much softer voice, "Sarge, are you hit?"

Pulling my hand out from under my body, I saw that it was covered with blood, and then I felt the warm trickles running down my face, and knew that this too was blood. Yes, I'd been hit, but all that I really felt was numb. Because my men couldn't see me clearly, they had no way of knowing if my legs had been blown off, or whether I was even still alive.

As the next volley of rounds went flying by, I wanted to yell at somebody to start shooting back, but I was afraid to make a sound. I was afraid to move. Afraid to move. Afraid to even breathe. The level of fear was so intense that I could only marvel at it. I would never have believed that a person's body could be this severely traumatized and still continue to function. And yet my heart continued to beat, my lungs continued to suck air, and I knew, that given the chance, I could still make a run for cover, and that my limbs would somehow manage to support me. In my mind I was already running a million miles per hour, running faster than anyone had ever run before, faster than the speed of sound, running on and on forever.

But no, I was there on the ground, and the gooks were still shooting, and no one was shooting back. No way out! They could riddle me with bullets if they wanted to, and pretty soon they would, and that would be the end of it. No more heroics. No more crazy ideals about bravery, and the love of country, and Audie Murphy standing twenty feet tall on the screen. This was the truth of it—not standing tall, but laying flat on the ground, with my butt in the air, waiting for a bullet to find its mark. The bullet with my name on it. I could see no way out of any of this. My guys weren't firing, and the enemy wouldn't stop. I had been expecting my entire life to flash before me, but it didn't. My mind had suddenly gone blank, and I was just waiting. Waiting, as I took another breath, and listened to my heart beat.

Then, a guy by the name of Herschel, suddenly fired a shot. After that, he fired another two or three rounds, and while he was doing that I quickly reacted. As I started to crawl in his direction, he stopped firing, possibly because he was so shocked to discover that I could move.

To shake him out of his stupor, I yelled, "Keep firing, you idiot!" and a few other things, which seemed to do the trick. As he started firing again, another guy named Collins, who was standing beside him, started firing as well.

Once Herschel and Collins had both opened up, I started crawling faster than I've ever crawled in my life. I felt as if I did a thousand yards in three seconds. I crawled past these two guys, who were firing, and once I felt reasonably safe, I grabbed my rifle and, that quickly, I was ready to fight. My gratitude at still being alive was momentarily repressed as I hurriedly assessed the situation. I was looking for twelve of my guys, who I eventually found huddled in a bunker with no top on it; they were just sitting there, obviously waiting for us to come back.

I started yelling at them about being pinned down under fire, and needing their help and asked them what the hell they thought they were doing.

One of them said, "Well, the fact is, we were taking fire from the trees, Sarge, and that's why we got in this bunker."

Gooks in the trees! Okay, I thought. So, now we have gooks in the trees. But, what the hell. Our job here was done. It was time to get back to the firebase.

As the men acted on this order, I went back to where Herschel and Collins were, and laid down another base of fire to give them the chance to retreat. In that way, we managed to work our way out.

It wasn't until they were all safely on their way back out of the area that the shock of the entire experience finally hit home. I felt suddenly nauseated, shaky and weak, and sweat was running off me like it was running out of a tap. I was dying of thirst, and gasping for breath, and my clothes were wringing wet.

Bracing myself against a tree, I gave into a spell of the dry heaves, and after that, leaned my forehead against the trunk of the tree. Then, just as I moved my head, the tree absorbed a sudden round of fire that was obviously meant for me.

Turning, I caught a glimpse of the enemy, and saw my chance— that split-second when he was poised between shots, or maybe he was out of bullets. I took quick aim and fired, and I didn't miss.

When he fell out of the trees, I didn't go over and check him out. I didn't want to see another dead man, with a family back home, lying in a twisted heap on the ground, with that agonized expression that comes with a painful death.

When I got back to the firebase, everyone immediately ran toward me, including Doc, who treated me quickly for a lot of superficial wounds. Superficial! The most beautiful word in the English language in the middle of a war.

While I was reporting in to my lieutenant, the other men all dispersed, and went back to building their bunkers for the night fight.

When I was told that I had earned myself a Purple Heart, I told the lieutenant to forget about it, but he had a counter-argument. What he said was, "Look, it isn't just a medal to wear on your uniform because it looks good. After this thing is over, it'll help you land any kind of civil service job, should you ever want one, and of course, it'll also have some bearing on the quality of military benefits you receive, including disability, if necessary."

Well, the word benefits sounded all right, but I didn't care for the sound of disability. After everything I'd been through, was it still reasonable to hope that I might get out of this war without being shot up so badly that I would be partially or even totally disabled? Maybe not, but who could say? Thus far, God had seemed to be on my side in every skirmish, although, in those days, I still had Him confused with Lady Luck, and usually addressed Him in this way.

That night, we got ourselves settled in for some night fighting. Jake Broderick, who was in charge of the first squad, went out to set up the ambush that night. As part of the second squad, I knew they wouldn't go out very far, preferring to stay inside the trip wires, which meant they were only about 50 feet away.

Sometime during the night, we heard them blow the claymores, and found out a little later that a bunch of gooks had walked into the ambush. It scared the men in Jake's squad so badly that they all came running back to the firebase, leaving their weapons and radio behind.

When the company commander ordered them to go back out and retrieve this equipment, Jake, their squad leader, went with them, since he was the only one who knew the exact location.

The whole time this was going on, we could still hear the gooks out there carrying on. We didn't know how large a unit we'd hit, or whether they would counter-attack or what. One of our options was to just start firing that way, but if we did that, we knew we would automatically give away our position. The dark of the moon was giving us an undeniable advantage, which we weren't exactly eager to relinquish.

Once a decision had been made to use the .90mm recoilless rifle, we suddenly realized that the gunner for this weapon was nowhere to be found. The assistant gunner was there, which meant we had someone who knew how to load the thing, but there wasn't anyone to shoot it. The next question, of course, was who could we use in a pinch?

It only took the lieutenant a few minutes to get around to me, and when he asked if I'd been trained on this weapon, I admitted that I had.

"And can you fire this weapon?" he asked.

"Yessir," I said.

With that, they laid down a base of security and I went out with this rifle, which was almost six feet long, and fired electrically. The assistant gunner accompanied me, and once we'd gotten the gun stationed in place, the assistant gunner opened the breech, slammed in a shell, and we were in business. As soon as I heard a sound, I fired, and after that, everything went deadly quiet.

Meanwhile, my assistant opened the breech, pulled out the casing, threw in another shell, and we were ready to fire again. I waited until I heard some more yelling and screaming, and then I fired again. I fired a total of three times, before crawling back to the firebase with my weapon. In the pitch blackness of night, I had no way of knowing if I had accomplished anything out there, but at least I had followed orders.

The next morning, at about 4:00 a.m., we were ready to go out and take a look around. Our scout, who spoke Vietnamese, informed the enemy that they were surrounded and that we would blow them all to Kingdom Come unless they agreed to surrender. It only took a few minutes for them to decide to throw in the towel, and as we moved in, I looked off toward the place where I'd positioned myself the previous night, and about 50 feet away, I saw a machine gun. Behind the machine gun were two dead men—the gunner, and the assistant gunner. The machine gun was locked and loaded, and I suddenly realized that the only reason I was still alive was because I had managed to get in a shot before they did.

I saw then that I had killed a total of four people, and because of the kind of weapon the recoilless rifle was, nearby trees were infested with fragments of human hair, flesh, brain matter and bone. A grisly sight in broad daylight!

In the previous 24 hour period, I had killed a total of five people in all. While some of my men congratulated me, I stood there thinking that I had actually made this decision concerning the lives of these humans, and that I had done this thing, and that whatever else I felt, I certainly didn't feel good about it.

What we ended up with were a total of nine dead, and three POWs, and four of those kills were mine.

After that, we continued to wander on through the jungle, looking for somebody to kill, but all we ever saw were a lot of bombed out trails.

General Westmoreland was supposedly given credit for the Checkerboard system of fighting, after realizing that he didn't have enough troops to totally saturate Vietnam.

A map was referred to as a "funny paper", and was divided into squares referred to as grids. So, one day, Westmoreland got the idea to set up the country like a checkerboard, and every area that was shaded in had an American unit on it. The point was to put each company in charge of 1,000 meters which would make it impossible for the gooks to totally infiltrate. While it was a good strategy in theory, there were a few holes in it, and the gooks were pretty clever at what they did, and so, a lot of them managed to get through.

Anyway, during one of the evening reports, we heard that a large body of gooks were headed our way, so we set up our ambushes and waited for them to arrive. Along about 9:00 p.m., we got a second report that reinforced the first. After, that, all the squad leaders met at the command post to discuss what they had heard.

Rumor had it that another company had seen 200 gooks go through on the trail of their ambush, but because they were so heavily outnumbered, they simply let them pass, and counted them as they went by.

What we were now being told was that these gooks were headed our way, and that we were bound to make contact with them sometime during the night.

A couple hours later, when the ambush was sprung, we killed a bunch of gooks, and the fight was on. However, no one fired a single rifle shot. We could hear them out there, but they weren't shooting. They obviously didn't want us to see them, and we certainly didn't want them to see us. So, what we did was toss out a bunch of hand grenades, and watch them explode in the darkness.

Occasionally, we heard some noise off in the distance, but nothing we could really identify. Finally, the lieutenant suggested I take the recoilless rifle and do what I'd done before.

As I crawled back out there, I got to thinking that this was really tempting fate. I thought about the gunner and his assistant behind the machine gun, and how easily they might have killed me before I'd had a chance to kill them. This situation was very much the same, but this time, the lucky shot might well be theirs.

I waited until I heard a noise, and another noise, and finally, I heard some gooks talking, and that's when I fired. I fired two more times and then I crawled back, and waited with the others until morning.

Shooting into a sea of total darkness can seem rather pointless, but this isn't really true with a gun that shoots a 3-inch round, covering an 8 to 10 foot space. This time we found three bodies, one man with his leg bandaged up, another guy who was probably their medic, and also, the guard for the medic. I'd killed all three with one shot. Two of the dead had their heads blown off.

The guy who did the killing always got the souvenirs—buttons off a dead man's uniform, or anything else that could possibly pass for a trophy. In this case, I found a photo in the pocket of one of the headless men—a picture of a man with two young children standing beside him. I looked at the picture and thought that the lives of two young people had just been changed forever. They would never see their father again, they would never know how he died, and would wonder all their lives about the circumstances surrounding his loss.

Although I did not know it at the time, that photo would haunt me the rest of my life. I often thought about, and even dreamed about those children, and also their mother, who probably had taken the picture, since she wasn't in the scene herself.

But there wasn't any time to think of these things on the morning following the assault. As we moved on up the trail, we found more wounded and dead, and many who lay dying. The body count was high, and three of them were mine.

It would later be referred to as a victorious battle in the bush, since we suffered no casualties of our own.

Chapter 4

Another aspect of war I hadn't quite counted on was the attitude we were expected to assume toward the enemy. For many, it wasn't always enough to kill men, or to take prisoners.

I saw incidents where people were so traumatized by their experiences, or by raw-boned fear, that they simply went ahead and died. Many of the men we captured were shaking uncontrollably at the thought of what might happen to them next. I didn't understand their fears at first, but after a while, I did.

I knew that people often died from shock that resulted from their wounds. This was commonplace, and only to be expected. But what I hadn't expected was the thrill-seeking that came out of torturing prisoners, or even mutilating the dead. As if the perpetrator were trying to kill these people twice. Ironically, everyone I knew who engaged in this kind of behavior, ended up dying themselves, except for one, who landed in the psychiatric ward.

As for me, I knew I was there to do a job, just as our enemies were, and once I had taken prisoners, I saw no reason to humiliate or torture them, since they were already humiliated and tortured by their own state of mind. To see anyone with a totally broken spirit is to see someone who represents no further threat. At this point, I felt it only right to give them food and water, and to protect the fragile shell that still remained of their bodies and their minds. After this was over, they would have to rely on whatever they had left, even as I would, to try to rebuild their lives.

At that time, I had no way of knowing that a single experience—one battle in particular—would follow me for the rest of my life. I did not know then that it would haunt my dreams, and also my waking hours, and make the fragile shell of my own psyche extremely difficult, if not impossible to live with.

I reflect upon it now, some thirty years later, and find it is still alive and well. There is no aspect of it that I have ever forgotten, and not because I haven't wanted to. If I could tear that part of my brain away, I would gladly do so.

It began as an ordinary day. The night before, we'd gotten drunk on the firebase and partied a bit—in other words, had ourselves a little fun.

The following morning we were saddled up by 5:30 but the choppers didn't come for us until eleven o'clock. It felt like an "easy day" to me because I didn't have that much to do. My squad was walking drag, which meant we were the farthest back, which suited me just fine. All I had to do that day was make sure that no one snuck up behind us.

The third platoon was checking out bunkers when we suddenly got word that there were gooks in the area. This had been preceded by a loud explosion, which is the way most major firefights began. All hell would break loose for a time, until suddenly, everyone on both sides stopped shooting. It was as if they were giving one another an opportunity to evaluate the situation, to estimate the damage, and to decide if they'd had enough. Then, a few minutes later, the fighting would begin again. Few movies about Vietnam depict this the way it really is.

Once things had settled down a bit, the message we received was to make up some stretchers and to send out the 2nd platoon because there was a need for reinforcements.

The sound of the second explosion was followed by another horde of green and red tracer bullets. The next message that came over the radio instructed us to keep making stretchers and advised that the 2nd platoon had nearly been wiped out. The next order we received was to send one squad of the first platoon down to help out.

It was then, that we realized how bad it was. Standard operating procedures always required that a platoon be kept in reserve. Things have really reached a serious state once the reserve platoon, or any portion of it, becomes committed.

Another message that came through: "Send one squad of the 1st platoon. Secure the area. Those that are back there, just start making stretchers and *don't quit.!*

I immediately began setting up security for the perimeter. Since my squad was walking rear security, I figured the lieutenant would take one of the other squads. I was wrong. Not only was my squad going, I was walking point.

By the time we were ready to go, a half-hour had passed, along with more volleys of gunfire from both sides.

Because the gooks had been jamming our radio transmissions, an elite top-secret team consisting of three people carrying special equipment came with us on this mission. We knew it was pretty sensitive stuff because two of the three were lieutenants. Since they had just joined us that morning, all we'd really had an opportunity to do was acknowledge their presence.

I had just started down the trail, when two of that three-man team came walking back. The point man, or private, was crying.

"God!" he said. "Whatever you do, don't go any further down this trail. They cut us to ribbons while we were trying to get out. They've got us locked in on a U-shaped ambush."

I looked at one of the lieutenants for confirmation. He was speechless, and as white as a ghost. We noticed then that he was carrying his rifle in his left hand and realized that his right hand had very nearly been blown off. The fact was, it was dangling on the end of his arm by a thin strip of skin.

My stomach churned at this gruesome sight and I fought hard to maintain my composure. We had been taught to act normally in situations of this kind—to act, not *react,* since this could easily set off a chain reaction. I found myself wondering if the man was thinking that the medics could reattach his hand, or if he was even aware of it.

Suddenly, I heard the lieutenant say, "Let's go, Sarge."

As I slowly came out of my daze, I got to thinking about the other lieutenant, and wondered if, he had been taken out by the .51 caliber. I wasn't able to give it any great amount of thought though since, of course, we still had the immediate situation to deal with.

With a U-shaped ambush, there are three options: 1. Fight your way out the way you got in. 2 Flank one side. 3. Flank both sides, if enough people are available.

On this particular day, the only choice was no. 2, and the obvious choice was the right flank since I preferred to face a .30 caliber weapon rather than a .51 caliber machine gun.

I cut about twenty or thirty feet over to the right, and started breaking brush with Vernon Howes, an ex-drill instructor who should have been a sergeant but who had been busted down. In my opinion, he was the perfect point man—compact and sturdy. At a distance, it was hard for the enemy to tell if he was a G.I. or a gook. Gooks were small, and so was Vernon, and their moment of hesitation often cost the enemy their lives.

Because I was so used to maneuvering my way through the jungle, I managed to get through without any problem. In the process, however, I lost contact with the rest of my squad, which was far in the rear.

I remember stepping over a wounded body lying on the ground, and when I looked closer, I saw that the victim's face was blue. I had never seen that before, and as I stood staring at him, I heard the Doc yell, "If we don't get this man out of here in the next five minutes, he's dead."

Within minutes after this statement was made, the wounded man died. Because he had gotten it in the face with a claymore mine, (one of our own), it took me a while to realize that this was my good friend, Benjamin Hayes, a fellow Okie that I had recently shared a few fond reminiscences with. While sitting on the edge of a bunker on the firebase only the night before, he and I had looked down at the lights of a small city. Gazing down from a mountaintop, it was easy to imagine that these were the lights of Oklahoma City, and we talked about how it would feel to fly home again and see those lights blinking out their welcome as the plane began its gradual descent.

At the time of his death, Benjie only had twenty-two days left to serve in Vietnam. He'd made it this far only to be hit by one of our own claymore mines.

The "easy day" I had imagined for myself had turned into a blood bath of such monumental proportions that it was difficult to describe, or even comprehend. There were bodies everywhere I looked—some dead, some dying—and some injured, who were determined to keep shooting until the world was flat.

The rifles they were using were literally smoking, and some became too hot to handle, and had to be dropped on the ground. When new magazines were inserted into these overheated chambers, they "cooked off" the rest of the rounds.

The 2nd platoon leader who had screamed so much at Lonnie Davis, my machine gunner friend, was also killed that day. He was the target of a direct hit from a B-40 rocket launcher (the second explosion), which took him out along with his RTO—giving new meaning to "he never knew what hit him."

Handing my cooler rifle to the guy who looked like he needed it the most, I went off to find a medic.

"What do we need to do?" I asked him.

"We need to get these guys out of here," he said.

After I located a radio, I sent out a call for some stretchers, and pretty soon I could see them coming down the trail. After that, it was simply a matter of picking up bodies where we found them. And they were everywhere we looked. Whenever a stretcher arrived, we would put a soldier on it, and send him to a holding or staging area.

I remember staring at these mounds of people and thinking that what I was seeing wasn't real—or if it was, that the entire world and everybody in it had gone insane.

The Doc and I began working together on those we found who were still alive. As I cut away their clothing, the Doc put a dressing on their wounds.

Keeping everyone's confidence up in a situation like this was very nearly impossible. The sight of this massacre was enough to shake anyone's faith in whatever cause we had once believed in, and there were many whose opinions and ideas about the war changed dramatically on that day.

Once our clean-up work was done, I took one look around, and that's when I saw another body in the bushes. In all the confusion, he had somehow been overlooked. His name was Herman Tripp, but we always called him the Bee-Man because of what he had told us about his lucrative bee business back in the states.

After I spotted him, I grabbed hold of the Doc's Medic bag before he had a chance to leave. We examined the Bee-Man's injuries and realized he had been hit with the same claymore mine. He'd been shot in the leg, and after cutting his pants with my knife, I attempted to apply a dressing I'd been carrying on my shoulder harness. As I started to tear the packet for this dressing open with my teeth, a shot rang out and I felt an excruciating pain in my hand.

Since the Doc was kneeling beside me, he grabbed my hand but I assured him that it was only a superficial wound and that we needed to get out of there. I called for a stretcher for the Bee-Man, and once it arrived, I attempted to carry one end, but my hand was hurting so badly, that I could barely bend my fingers. At the same time, I was suddenly overwhelmed with thirst.

Turning the stretcher over to a private who was standing nearby, I moved off, with my hand bleeding profusely, and joined a team of men who were working with the dead. We covered them with ponchos and lifted them onto stretchers. As the stretchers were being carried down the trail, one of the ponchos suddenly became caught on a wait-a-minute vine. These vines had thorns in them, similar to rose bushes, but the thorns were more like fishhooks, and when they snagged anything, it was necessary to "wait a minute" while you backed up, since that was the only way to work the hook free.

When the wait-a-minute vine caught on the dead man's poncho, it was pulled back, exposing the body for the stretcher carriers to see. One of these men reacted with immediate shock when he recognized the dead man as a young kid he had come in country with two or three weeks earlier.

As soon as he recognized his dead friend, he began shaking uncontrollably. Walking over to him, I slapped him hard with my good hand. I slapped him twice, just like they did in the movies. First, I gave him an open-handed slap, and then I back-handed him. After that, I reached down, grabbed him by the shirt and shook him until I had his full attention. Pointing to his dead friend as they were putting the poncho back on the stretcher, I said, "If you don't want to end up like your friend here, you'd better get your rifle and start laying down a base of fire so that we can get the hell out of here!"

He looked up at me, and sort of grabbed at my words as he quickly nodded his head. "Yeah! That's right. Okay, Sarge!" he said, and immediately began following orders.

When we got back to the main area, I ran into a guy named Gray Parson, who only had about fifteen days left in country. He'd been hit by the claymore mine too and had some superficial wounds on his legs. He was lying on the ground with his eyes closed, when somebody came along and stepped on him.

At that, Gray opened his eyes, and said, "Hey, you do that again, and I'll kill you."

I remember thinking that here was a man in the midst of all this devastation as cool and self-possessed as anyone could possibly be. He was acting like someone who'd just been roused out of an afternoon nap, and he wasn't at all happy about it. At this point, we had ourselves a trail leading out of the kill-zone, and it was time to go back out. Looking over toward the company commander, I saw that he'd been hit and that his rifle had been blown to bits. Even so, he was on the radio, reporting in to the battalion commander, and he seemed to be functioning well.

Approaching a guy named Buzz, I said, "Okay you walk point." He was sitting on the ground and just continued to sit there.

"So. You gonna walk point or what?" I asked, in an effort to get him to move.

"Hell, Sarge, just look at me," he said, and I watched as he wiggled his foot. There was blood squishing through his battered boot, and I knew then that he couldn't walk.

"All right," I said, and apologized. Since I only had an injured hand, I decided that I would walk point. I knew where the firebase was, so I started out, but I was still dying of thirst, and before I had gone very far, I was already feeling exhausted.

When I reached an open area, I knew the base was just ahead. I wanted to call out to some of my men, but then I remembered that there was a .51-caliber set up on that trail. There was also a bomb crater, and when I finally reached it, I just sort of fell down inside.

Since I had gotten so far ahead of the men who were walking behind me with stretchers, I knew I had a little time to rest. Sitting at the bottom of the bomb crater, I looked up toward the sun, and my eyes came to rest upon a figure standing at the edge of the crater. The shadowy figure didn't move, and neither did I; we just silently appraised each other.

I knew who it was, and it seemed to know me. The infamous Death Angel was paying another call.

Sometime earlier, a G.I. by the name of Jack Bridges, after seeing the Death Angel had written a letter home, and his parents were appalled at its tone. It was written by a man who seemed to have already died, and it offered no hope of any homecoming.

A few days later, his parents received this letter along with a Death Notice from the Army.

As I lay there staring up at the Death Angel, I felt a sudden urge to postpone what appeared to be the inevitable, and so, I began clawing my way out of the bomb crater. The loose silt made it difficult to get a firm footing, but I finally reached the top and quickly scrambled out.

As I paused to rest, I saw another soldier approaching, and started crawling toward him on my hands and knees. When I reached him, he handed me his LRRP canteen, and so, I finally got a drink of water, and told him we were all coming back to guide the others in.

Once we'd all managed to get back to our firebase, we sent out a fresh squad to secure an area where a helicopter could land to take out our wounded.

As luck would have it, we had more wounded than we had Medivacs, so the men were taken out six at a time, which made it seem like it was taking forever.

I was never so glad to leave a place, believing perhaps that escaping from there would also make it possible for me to escape from what I had seen.

We were taken to our battalion firebase where they were set up like a little M.A.S.H. unit to give us more medical attention.

Gray Parsons, who had appeared to be napping comfortably a little earlier that day, suddenly called out to one of the medics. "Hey, Doc, I don't feel so good."

The Doc checked him out and said, "Hell, it's just your wounds that are making you uncomfortable." He gave Gray a shot of morphine, and that seemed to settle him down for awhile. A while later, though, he complained that he couldn't catch his breath, and by then, his respiration and pulse rate had dropped dramatically.

By then, my hand had been bandaged, so I decided to see if I could help. Having worked in a hospital emergency room for a year, I was the closest thing to a medic, and so, I often assisted the Doc.

When I took Gray's pulse, I could only count sixteen beats a minute. At that point, I gave him some mouth to mouth, trying to keep him alive. He was still breathing when the chopper arrived, but when he got up where the air was cooler, and where there wasn't anyone to assist him with his breathing, he gasped his last and died.

The question of what had actually happened to Gray remained a mystery until we learned he had gotten high on cocaine while he was waiting for the choppers to pick us up. This meant that when the Doc gave him a shot of morphine, he had actually O.D.ed the poor guy.

As for me, I was struggling along with my hand. It was giving me a great deal of trouble for a superficial wound, although I was careful how I used it. I kept it wrapped, and tried to think about other things, but it was swelling, and the pain was becoming excruciating. Drinking didn't seem to help. And neither did my pain pills. By the third day I couldn't stand it any longer, and although the Doc had a lot of others to attend to, I finally hunted him down and asked if there was anything he could do.

He unwrapped my hand and took a good look at it. "Damn!" he said. "It looks like gangrene is getting ready to set in. We'd better send you back to the rear and have a medic take care of this."

The doctor I saw seemed equally alarmed and told me to check into the hospital.

Once I had done this, an operation was scheduled for the following day. Meanwhile, I ran into the Doc in the mess hall and when I told him how everything had been arranged, he said, "I don't' think we have that much time. We'd better perform that operation today. You go ahead and have lunch and then we'll get right on it."

Although I wasn't really looking forward to this, I didn't want to lose my hand, so I figured I'd better go along with what the Doc was saying.

What they ended up doing was laying me down in a chair with leather straps attached to it, which reminded me a little of an electric chair. Once the straps had been secured in all the proper places, the Doc said, "We've got one little problem here, Sarge. The 'bird' hasn't gotten here yet with all the supplies I ordered, which means I don't have any pain-killers to give you. And we can't wait any longer on this. What I'm going to do is give you this little piece of plastic to put between your teeth. Whenever the pain gets really bad, just bite down hard. I'm sorry, but that's the best I can do."

While I was still thinking about this, the Doc cut a hole in my hand big enough to insert his instruments, and after that, I started feeling like the top of my head was going to blow off. At some point, I decided I would kill this doctor as soon as I had the chance. And while I thought about a lot of different ways of doing it, the operation continued. Taking his knife, the Doc started scraping the bone in my hand, and all the infected tissue, which he later doused with something that might have been hydrogen peroxide. It felt warm, and caused me more pain.

I spent some time in the hospital after that, with liquid penicillin I.V.s running into both arms. My stay in the hospital gave me some time to think, which forced me to confront some major questions in my mind. The largest question, of course, concerned itself with whether or not I still believed in what we were doing.

At the outset, it had been my feeling, and the feeling of most of the men, that we were doing something good in Vietnam. Our main objective was not to kill, but rather to save lives. We were there to defend freedom, and to give a new nation an opportunity to grow. The south Vietnamese were entitled to freedom and independence, and we had hoped to help them achieve it.

We had no illusions about the cost involved, since every war has shown us its price tag. Personal sacrifice and a strong sense of responsibility directed by certain values and principles are necessary if we hope to give a voice. Although we did not enter this war with the thought of imposing our own views on anyone, we still felt responsible for the human rights of every human being, and wanted to do what we could to insure the freedoms and liberties that our own country had always enjoyed.

Even as a child, I had felt something that bordered on this when I thought about such words as heroes, and patriotism, and winning. It was all wrapped up somehow in Mom's apple pie, the Statue of Liberty, and the American flag. Whatever it all stood for always gave me a warm and cozy feeling. It felt right, and good, and like something that everyone in the world should want, and also be entitled to.

But out here in the swamps, in the midst of an ambush in the jungle, or while firefighting, or facing the enemy dead-on, it seemed to me that something had gotten lost. It might have been the cause, or it might have been me, but something was definitely missing.

I didn't feel what Audie Murphy had felt, or seemed to be feeling on his road *To Hell and Back*. That feeling of triumph or accomplishment seemed determined to elude me, and in its place, there was only a kind of gray depression.

I had watched my buddies fight and die for no apparent reason. As for me, I had managed to survive thus far, but not without the growing suspicion that we might actually be the losers in a misconceived war.

But could I really afford to question the unquestionable? If this was, in fact, a war without valid meaning or objective, then what were we doing here, and why should we even continue? As time went on, I was becoming increasingly confused about whether or not the war actually had anything to do with Communism or Democracy. And if it didn't, then what were those bodies of the dead and injured all about? Those terrorized looks, those glazed eyes, those mouths twisted and frozen in death's final grimace—for what had these men suffered and died?

These were the youngest American soldiers to have fought in any war, the average age being 19.2 years as compared to 26 years in World War II. At such a tender age, they were ill-prepared for the carnage and terror they experienced, oftentimes, within days after they were flown in.

In my own case, I could remember feeling uprooted, transplanted and also dislocated, as if I'd been left on some alien planet. Vietnam, with its strange language, and its unfamiliar habits and customs, made me feel lost and alone. We were forced to grow up in a single day, and to rely upon coping skills and strategies that we didn't actually possess. We observed and copied what others were doing, but deep down inside, the Vietnam experience was different for every one of us, depending on each soldier's personality and value system.

The overwhelming tension of war—particularly the dreaded fear of being "blown away"—had to be dealt with on a daily basis. Drugs and alcohol were the handiest solutions—something that aided in sleeping, and mind-numbing, and anesthezing emotions and memories—at least for a time.

I had begun to wonder about the long-range effects of what we were experiencing, since I knew that any mind-altering substance was only a temporary solution at best. Out in the jungle, there was little time to think, but here in the hospital, it was easy enough to play it all back, like a movie in my mind. I remembered it all— every name, and face, every anguished cry, every terrifying sound in the night. Instant recall! Almost anything could trigger it.

Time and distance. I had heard that these were the best antidotes. Once I went home, life would become what it had always been, and the Vietnam experience would begin to seem like a bad dream. Wouldn't it?

It was a question I had no answer for. I sensed that something inside me was gradually changing, that I was different in ways that friends and family would undoubtedly notice. But what was the name for this thing I had become?

I had killed people now. I had killed them, and also *watched* them being killed, and after that, I had eaten and slept, and functioned quite normally, in a way I would never have believed possible. I had come to accept the unacceptable, and now it was altogether ordinary. But what did that make *me?*

The next time a doctor came in to check on me, I asked him how soon I could leave. He took it as an encouraging sign, not realizing that I was merely desperate to escape my own thoughts.

Once the Doc had given me my release papers, with two weeks back in the rear while my hand was healing, I headed for our rear echelon headquarters, where I learned that my request to transfer from NO DEROS DELTA to a Recon team had been approved.

While I was extremely pleased about this, I also knew that I would be leaving some really great guys behind. I was reminded of this when I started running into a number of them who had been wounded in the same firefight, and who were recuperating from their own wounds. For awhile, it was almost like a homecoming.

When I ran into the guy I'd slapped back to his senses, I figured he'd want to take advantage of my injured hand and really kick some butt, but he turned out to be the friendliest one in the bunch.

After offering me a beer, he said, "Hey Sarge, I want to thank you for what you did for me. If you hadn't, I'd probably end up just like Shakey there."

Shakey, as he had come to be known, was a soldier who had totally lost it. At some point, all the suffering and death got to him, and he just started crying in a way that made us all wonder if he was ever going to stop. He kept saying that he knew he was going to die too, and then he got the shakes, and that's when everybody started calling him Shakey. The "lifers" gave him a pretty hard time, assigning him to all the dirtiest details, and sometimes they even snuck up on him at night to see if he also shook in his sleep. When they saw that he did, they eased up on him a bit. It was funny to watch him smoke at night because of the way the lighted tip of his cigarette would dance around like a nervous firefly. Shakey was really a good guy, and although he'd never fired a shot, he was definitely one of the walking wounded, scared for his life. He lived from one day to the next, just waiting for his medical discharge to come through.

The final count that day was 43 men wounded and five dead. Two of the casualties were from Oklahoma. There had been five Okies in that company to begin with—now two were dead, one had been wounded and sent back to the States, one derosed, and then there was me—the one who'd been transferred.

A question that had been plaguing us for a while got answered that day, namely: Where did the gooks get the claymore mines that took out so many of our guys?

What we eventually learned was that one of our sister companies had previously made contact with this same bunch of gooks, and once they started fighting, this company left their rucksacks behind, with no one to guard them. The gooks had then come in behind them and taken everything, including the claymore mines.

This was the kind of stupidity that made me eager to join up with a Recon unit. Before I left, the guys let me know that they were sorry to see me go, and told me that the company commander had requested that I be awarded a Silver Star for what I had accomplished that day.

Chapter 5

For a long time, we had been hearing that Recondo School was unlike anything else in the history of the military, since the training that it gave to its graduates endowed them with the skills to survive Long Range Patrol missions in jungles that the NVA considered its own. The LRRPs had been trained to win, and nothing else was acceptable.

The human senses were elevated to a level far beyond our normal imaginings since, in the jungles of Vietnam, so much depended on them.

We soon realized that much valuable information could be gained about the enemy, just by smelling, looking, touching and listening.

A sense of smell was particularly important on those dark and moonless nights when we couldn't see two feet in front of us. At such times, we learned to smell the air, much as an animal does. We could often smell the enemy before we could actually see him, and the way in which this applied to obtaining and developing combat intelligence was to give us some clue, not only to what he was doing now, but to what he had been doing in the past.

Cigarette smoke can be detected up to one-quarter mile if wind conditions are exactly right. It is also possible to smell the aroma of certain foods when they are being cooked, primarily fish and garlic. If the enemy is close enough, you can even detect the presence of a man who has been *eating* these foods, and in this way, discover a guerrilla ambush before your patrol has made the mistake of walking into it.

In Vietnam, where many types of wood were used for fuel, we were trained to identify all of these aromas, since this could help to determine the general location of the fire, the guerrilla camp, or patrol base.

The smells of soap, after-shave lotion, or other such toiletry articles, were also easily detected, especially by those who weren't in the habit of using such things.

Finally, it was also possible to detect the smell of explosives, which would cling to the clothing and the hands of those who had been working with them.

Moving on to a sense of touch, we quickly discovered its importance on those occasions when we were forced to search buildings, tunnels, or enemy corpses in the dead of night. During the dark of the moon or when lights could not be used for security reasons, we often identified an object by touch, based on four major considerations: shape, moisture, temperature, and texture.

A good example of this was the timely detection of trip wires, which was sometimes done by holding a very fine branch in front of us. We could feel if it struck anything.

Of course, hearing was a sense we all quickly learned to "fine tune" in the jungle. The sound of a safety latch being released on a rifle or machine gun could warn of an ambush or a sniper. And the sound of wild birds suddenly taking flight could be an indication of enemy movement. Then too, dogs barking often warned us that we were approaching a village.

Of course, we had also been trained to listen for 'opposite' sounds, when birds and dogs became suddenly still. This often meant that the enemy had passed.

The trick was to move cautiously enough so that we could hear sounds made by the enemy without making any noticeable sounds ourselves.

It was also extremely important to determine the range of enemy weapons and to identify their type and caliber.

Recondo teams were taught to respond to the sound of an enemy weapon in specific ways. One was to rotate the upper body, with the hands cupped around the ears. The object was to find in which direction the sound registered the loudest since this was obviously its point of origin.

Another factor to be considered was that, without wind, air currents generally flowed downhill at night and uphill in daylight. Also, when the wind was to our back, dogs would sometimes bark to warn of our approach, which was something a good tracker constantly had to keep in mind.

Tracking, of course, was an art in itself. We were constantly on the lookout for the displacement or disturbance of soil, vegetation or wildlife. Footprints could indicate several things: the number of people in a party, the direction in which they were moving, their sex, and in some cases, the type of load they were carrying. Prints were studied for signs that could be recognized again—worn or unworn heels, cuts in the heels, tread patterns, and also, the angle of the impression from the direction of movement.

A person carrying a heavy load would usually leave prints that were normally spaced, with exceptionally deep toe prints. Sometimes, we would see signs where the load had been placed on the ground during a rest break. Someone who was exceptionally adept at reading footprints could tell when a load had been dropped, which meant there were gooks in the area and that we needed to search for a cache or some underground tunnels.

Vegetation that had been disturbed in some way was either dragged out of place, or when the branches were broken, would reveal lighter colored undersides. Vines were often broken and dragged parallel to or toward the direction of movement. Grass, when stepped on, would usually bend toward the direction of movement, and when the bark on a log or root had been scuffed, the lighter, inner wood would show, leaving an unmistakable sign.

It was also not uncommon to run across shreds of cloth, or to find threads or bits of clothing clinging to the underbrush, particularly if movement had been hurried.

All the while, we were constantly on the lookout for bloodstains, and soil displacement caused by footgear. The color and composition of the soil could indicate a previous location or route over which an enemy party had moved.

The muddying of normally clear water was a sign of very recent movement which was easily detected by any trained eye.

Littering was not common since it could only be the result of total ignorance, but occasionally, some small shred of evidence would be left behind: cigarette butts, scraps of paper and cloth, match sticks, ration cans, and even abandoned equipment.

Patrol techniques had been well thought out, and we had considerable opportunity to review them as we waited in the dark for something to happen. Among other things, we had been taught to make a thorough map study and to always select an alternate rallying point.

We were told to always test-fire our weapons before going out on a mission but once this was done, we were not to tear them apart or clean them again.

We used silent hand signals as much as we possibly could, and were always encouraged to practice all hand and arm signals prior to departing on a mission.

Each night, we would put up field-expedient antenna and preset the artillery frequency on our radio. We would also periodically change our point man and compass man on long patrols, and were instructed to always carry our weapons pointed in the direction in which we were looking. Although this rule seemed like little more than common sense, the fact was, logic could evaporate in a moment when men were under attack, and I often saw guns pointed straight up in the air with bullets flying everywhere.

Sleeping was difficult in the jungle, and, more often than not, we managed it in snatches. If a man had difficulty in staying awake, he was told to kneel rather than sit. We were also urged to sleep close enough to touch each other, and to put handkerchiefs in our mouths if we had a tendency to snore.

We had been warned that unoccupied houses might contain booby traps, and to be cautious of all civilians. We tried never to set any kind of pattern with our activities, and *always* expected an ambush.

If ambushed, it was important to pick a single point and attack, and to never return over the same route.

On hard ground, we walked toe to heel. On soft ground, we walked flatfooted.

In a sudden engagement it was best to fire low, since a ricochet was better than no hit at all.

My main problem with what we had been doing in the past was that so much of it wasn't working. I had no quarrel with the theory involved, but it was a different matter once that theory was reduced to numbers.

By now, I had decided that making contact and fighting all the time, in the way we were going about it just wasn't my forte. Trying to root these people out of a bunker complex when they were already dug in, particularly when you didn't have a lot of men to do it with, was a suicide mission at best. We usually ended up calling in the bombs and big guns because we just weren't winning.

The Cherokee side of my nature was instinctively drawn to the Recon team, because it gave me a better opportunity to work in a solitary fashion, and to use my natural tracking skills. I had been told that these groups were small, that they provided better support, and that I would be able to avail myself of the tactics and strategy that reflected my own best judgment.

I had a real knack for reading the woods, and because of a highly developed intuition, I sensed things and saw things that most people missed. I also had a knack for moving through the jungle and sneaking up on people without being noticed, and I knew how to protect myself.

The Indian in me was rather intrigued by the meaning behind the recon insignia, which each member of the team wore while in Vietnam. It was an arrowhead, pointing downward, which symbolized the air-to-ground methods of infiltration into enemy territory, and was further representative of the American Indian skills of field craft and survival.

The physical training the Recon team participated in also included a lot of running. The runs were killers, each one longer than the first, building up to a torturous nine-miler. What made each run so grueling was that it was always done with full combat gear: rifle, six quarts of water, sixteen magazines—and a forty pound sandbag placed in a rucksack.

It was easy enough to recognize a Recondo graduate by the burn marks under his armpits and on his lower back. Running with that forty-pound rucksack could wear the skin right off.

As part of the Recon team, I began carrying more ammunition than what I was accustomed to, simply because there were less of us. Another thing that was different was that we only got supplied every five days, and this meant that I had to start carrying thirteen quarts of water, rather than only four. At eight pounds to the gallon, this represented a considerable increase, when added to all the other provisions that had to be taken along.

The first day, we went out, set up an ambush, killed ourselves two or three gooks and that was all there was to it. Because we were a scout team, we had been given an Indian name; they called us Big Sioux.

After awhile, the NVA decided they were going to mortar our firebase, but since the base was at the top of a mountain, the mortar rounds couldn't reach us and simply made a lot of noise.

Even so, we were duty-bound to go out and find the perpetrators, and as it happened, we had a pretty good idea where they were.

To get there, we had to cross an open field. Since I was walking point, I was the first to reach this area, and since we were spread out pretty good, I was about 50 feet away from the nearest guy.

I had moved out about one hundred and fifty feet when the enemy suddenly opened up on me with an AK 47 and a B-40 rocket. I saw the muzzle flash of the rifle and actually saw the rocket heading toward me. I hit the dirt and watched as the rocket exploded about fifteen feet away. Although I was hit with some shrapnel, I was still able to fight, and quickly crawled back to the tree line while my team laid down some cover fire. This incident earned me my third Purple Heart.

After the Doc had taken care of my wounds, we called in the gunships since we now had map coordinates of the enemy's position.

This was a small force. Only two people fired at us. If they'd known what they were doing, they'd have climbed a tree and waited for the whole team to get into the clearing and then pick a few of us off before we had a chance to get any support. As it was, we now each knew the other's position.

Although we did not get a body count that day, we did manage to find their main trail, so, we knew it was just a matter of time before we would encounter these gooks again.

The Battalion Commander was determined to get a body count before he brought us back in. We had been out over 40 days now, and were just as anxious to kill something as he was anxious to have us do it.

The rationale was that it was the gooks', fault for having brought this on, since they were the only reason we were even out there. So, okay—let's do it! Man-to-man, one-on-one. Killing somebody before they killed you meant the only thing it *could* out here—it meant you were the best, the very best there was in this game of Life or Death.

By now, I had become an expert at setting up ambushes, and along with everyone else, I was sick to death of C-rations, and the way we all looked and smelled. Even so, we were like a finely tuned machine. It had reached a point where we could anticipate one another's moves, and read each other's minds.

I had picked a perfect spot for an ambush. There was a bend in the trail which quite naturally caused the point man to focus on what was around that bend, rather than concentrating on the trail itself.

I laid a trip flare wire across the trail, in a spot where I felt it would not be so easily noticed. The wire was green and the ground was brown, which meant that sunlight could easily expose it, but only an amateur would make that kind of mistake. After studying the trail, I zeroed in on the perfect spot, thinking all the while that whoever walked into this would pay for the deaths of people like Davis, and Bridges, and Gray. That was how I kept myself psyched up for killing, how I kept myself primed, and ready to strike out at a moment's notice. When I was in the proper frame of mind, it felt good to kill, and while this was something I hadn't quite counted on, I knew it had a lot to do with staying alive. In order to care about anything out here, you had to "get pumped", and think in terms of "scoring" rather than taking people's lives.

That was the way I was thinking as I laid out my trip wire at a 45-degree angle in a shaded area, where the sun wouldn't cause it to glisten. Next, I carefully positioned three claymore mines—the first pointing straight back down the trail, the second as far back down the trail as the wire would reach and finally, the third one, the killer—which was connected to the others with wire I quickly spliced together. This one went down the trail about 100 feet—to the edge.

Experience had taught me that gooks maintained a certain distance from one another—at least three feet. Once the point man trips the flare, he knows he's in trouble. Everybody soon learns that the best way out of an ambush is the way they got in, but there's a certain amount of reaction time involved. First, the various options have to be considered, then a decision is made, and finally, some action is taken.

What usually happens is that the point man will run into the second man in the column, and then, these two try to persuade the rest to turn around and run. But, by this time, the ambusher has usually caught up with the ambushee. I figured that by having three claymores covering an area of over 150 feet, the enemy's chances of beating the odds were slim to none.

That day, when the trip flare popped, the claymores blew, and that quickly, there were three dead gooks. One managed to get away despite his injuries, probably because another soldier caught all the shrapnel from one of the mines.

Victory, sweet victory! We called our commander, fully expecting to be extracted and taken back to the firebase for some hot food and beer. Going back also meant showers and shaves, clean clothes, a few new faces, and—rest.

Unfortunately, the message that came back was that we were to undertake a new mission, which required that we stay where we were and ambush the bodies. Although we were highly displeased with these orders, we had little choice but to obey them.

"Stay out one more day!" we were told, and that was what we did.

Gooks rarely left their dead behind so we knew they'd be back. It was just a matter of time. Also, since one had gotten away, we knew he would be able to inform the other of the exact location of the bodies.

One final point. One of the gooks we killed had our M-79 grenade launcher and ammo, which he'd undoubtedly gotten from an American G.I. he'd killed. Tit-for-tat, I thought. It was a little like finding a dead Indian with a lot of white men's scalps on him. Needing to feel good about the people I killed, that was one way I had of justifying it.

I decided that our battalion commander had made the right decision. In war, humanity had to take a back seat. Besides, three of my best friends were dead, and three gooks for three G.I.'s just didn't settle the score. Besides, hadn't I almost lost my hand?

Webster's definition of the word *tactics* occasionally conflicted with our own. While the dictionary referred to *the technique or science of gaining objectives,* we were more inclined to think in terms of turnabout being fair play.

Remaining in the area after pulling off a successful ambush was not exactly normal procedure, especially with a unit as small as ours. Then too, ambushing bodies was a pretty morbid thing to be doing, but we knew that the gooks had done it with the bodies of our boys, and we were determined to return the favor.

We moved down the trail and set up another ambush. Our strategy was that the gooks would have to come through us to get to their dead.

Several hours passed, and during that time, we were reinforced with six new FNG's, including a machine gunner, who were certainly a welcome surprise. If the gooks were some distance away, and saw the choppers leaving, they might think we had abandoned the area, and decided to come around.

Nothing happened that night, but I remained tense and nervous, knowing that a fight was inevitable. The uncertainty that came with not knowing when something was going to happen kept my nerves on edge.

By 5:00 a.m. the next morning, the ominous stillness was beginning to wear on my patience. We were spread out on the trail, ready for a frontal or flank attack. To our rear, was a large open area. Not knowing how large a unit we would have to face merely added to the suspense.

Like good hunters, we finally went out to check our traps, and boy were we ever surprised! The gooks had walked up to our ambush, spotted the trip flare wire, stopped, and left. This could only mean one thing. They were going back for reinforcements.

The wire the gooks had spotted had been placed there by someone other than me, and when we reported in to our lieutenant, and told him what we had found, he made the best decision of his life by ordering us to reset our ambush.

After I'd done this, I laid down another trip wire, feeling, even as I did so, that we were being watched. My sixth sense was on red alert, and I remember that the radio man and I made a bet as to when we'd be hit. He said 10:30, and I said 10:00.

At 10:05, just as I was putting a letter away, the trip flare popped. Diving for the detonators, I blew the claymores. After a few moments of silence, we could hear some crying and moaning. Bingo! We'd gotten ourselves some bodies.

We were about to check things out when the enemy suddenly hit our left flank. Then they hit us in front, and then on the right, where we'd sprung the ambush.

Thus far, we had managed to hold our own, but this was about to change. We realized we were very nearly surrounded, and that there were a lot more of them than there were of us. The new FNG's were all scared out of their wits, but the old-timers took it in stride. It actually gave them a "rush"

Watching the FNG's made me realize how much we had over-come in the past few months. After holding off the enemy until we were nearly out of ammo, we called for reinforcements. The mes-sage that came back ordered us to get ready to retreat to a wooded area in the middle of the clearing. This would give us clear fields of fire, if the gooks came after us. But first, we had to wait for the command post and the other squad to pack up. What idiocy! I found myself thinking. After all, they'd had the *entire morning* to pack up.

When everybody was finally ready, a small team went out to make sure there weren't any gooks waiting for us. I was relieved when we received an "all clear" since, by then, all I had left were 16 magazines, and 50 rounds of machine gun ammo.

As a member of a Recon team, I soon learned that other soldiers sometimes thought of us as "gutsy to the point of craziness". Even so, we were always given priority. All artillery provided support, along with a helicopter gunship.

With the gooks closing in on us, the gunship hovered overhead, dropping hot gun links and extracted cartridges down on us. Boy, they were really hot! Still. It was better than dying.

Realizing it was time for us to leave the area, I pulled the C.S. gas grenade, just to make sure they didn't follow us. By now, we had the support of the whole world behind us, and we'd received word that reinforcements were on their way.

Once these reinforcements had arrived, we went out one more time, and found the bodies of the initial ambush. I was given credit for four kills—one of them a hardcore Vietnamese, a "lifer". He was old, clean-shaven, with a lifer's haircut. He had a mirror and razor in his pocket. Looking at him, I envisioned someone killing my grandfather and thought about how this would make me feel.

Meanwhile, I realized that the others were talking about me as if I were a hero, and when we got back to the firebase, I got the red carpet treatment for killing seven more gooks, with only one wounded G.I.

It was a good ratio in everybody's eyes, and ratios seemed to be what it was all about.

I tried to feel good about this, but I kept thinking about the old gook I had killed, and, down through the years, he would continue to haunt me in my dreams.

At such times, I often wondered how far I had actually progressed beyond my initial reactions to Vietnam.

At relatively safe entry points from the States, new GI's were often subjected to the sounds of loud and heavy shell bombardments. This was often their first taste of what lay ahead, but because they hadn't expected it so soon, they were always badly shaken up.

At such places as Cam Ranh Bay, these bombardments were actually coming from American weapons in an anti-enemy military exercise called H & I (Harassment and Interdiction). H & I fire was basically employed to scare off the enemy and to discourage their advancement.

In an effort to quiet their jangled nerves, new GI's would congregate in clusters at reception centers, wondering aloud what Vietnam was going to be like. They wondered about their commanding officers, their noncommissioned officers, and the front-line soldiers, or fellow grunts. They also wondered whether or not they would leave Vietnam alive.

In an effort to dissipate their fears, they often told jokes or the hair-raising war stories they had heard from a brother, a cousin, or friend who had written home about their own Vietnam experiences. After a day or two of swapping these stories, their anxiety levels began to rise, particularly as the moment of their departure to their units drew near.

Some new soldiers were literally hit hard by reality on their way to their unit. The transport trucks in which they were riding were sometimes attacked, kamikaze style, by VC sapper teams that had been commissioned to kill Americans at all costs.

Arriving at their assigned combat units, the new soldiers were often regarded suspiciously by the "older", more seasoned troops, who immediately adopted a kind of wait-and-see attitude toward them. Confronted with distrust and open hostility, the new soldiers knew they would have to prove themselves at the first opportunity, which sometimes led to foolish or even fatal errors in judgment.

Having been labeled greenhorns, green troops, or just fucking new guys, the new entrants had to work extremely hard to keep themselves psyched up, and their anxieties down. And even as the more seasoned soldiers continued to regard them as a source of constant worry, they also sought them out as a source of eagerly awaited news from home.

FNG's were especially avoided by the "short-timer:—a soldier with two or less months to serve. "Short-timers" was a term that soon became synonymous with "Careful and Cautious".

New recruits never forgot their first firefight, and frequently admitted that it was not only frightening, but also extremely embarrassing. An adult male is never quite prepared to lose all bladder and bowel control—and yet that can happen in a matter of minutes once the shooting starts. Once Charlie had them pinned down and was hitting them with everything he had, the shooting could go on for hours. In some cases, it didn't end until a call was finally put in for some napalm and bombers.

This is a pretty tough initiation for any new recruit to undergo, particularly when all he knows about it thus far is based on second-hand information.

To see the arm or the head of a comrade blown off in battle is enough to insure a lifetime of nightmares. Soldiers witnessing such scenes will often start vomiting, screaming, or crying uncontrollably. Their lack of control is as frightening to them as the scene itself, for they realize they have reached their limit early on, and may have nothing in reserve once the so-called "real fighting" starts.

Lonely, helpless and scared are words that most accurately describe what a soldier is feeling at a time when he had hoped to be feeling confident, courageous and strong. I remember that we would all look at each other, trying to see the fear in one another's eyes, which seemed important, as a means of justifying our own.

"First kills" in Vietnam were extremely hard to deal with. It didn't help that this was the enemy. We still felt guilty as hell, and would beat ourselves up about it—until, at last, military reality began to overpower civilian reality. Once this profound transformation in personality had taken place, it became much easier to do what we had come to Vietnam to do. Our psychic realignment eventually led to the acceptance of all manner of atrocities—and to a feeling that we were little more than "walking dead" to the extent that our emotions had become so incredibly numbed. How else was it possible to fight a war that was centered, in terms of its success, on body count rather than the traditional spoils of war—land, weapons and prisoners?

I remember too that officers entering combat units were observed with the same amount of suspicion and distrust accorded FNG grunts. Some of us would take it upon ourselves to closely watch the naïve "greenhorn" lieutenants before the battle began, to see how "together" they were. We figured it might well be up to us to prevent them from attempting to win the war single-handedly. In an effort to be heroes, we knew they could make the kind of rash decisions that could get us all killed. All too often, young lieutenants didn't protect their men and were viewed as unreliable, and potentially dangerous.

Once the war was over, many men said that had their leaders been more adept in the jungle, or more receptive to logic and reason, fewer of their buddies would have been killed, and their own injuries would not have been as severe and possibly, would not even have occurred. True or not, these sentiments were real for the men who were there. And for those with prolonged frustration and disappointment over what they perceived as poor leadership, there developed a kind of impotent anger.

Violent acts in Vietnam occasionally took the form of "American-against-American", the most frequent form being the "fragging" of officers and NCOs by their troops. Fragging was an assault on a superior through the use of fragmentation grenades.

Yes, it was a hard initiation for everyone. No one was spared, no one escaped the terror and the pain, and afterwards, no one was ever quite the same.

Chapter 6

After moving on to another (AO), Area of Operation, we set up a firebase with the help of a bulldozer and some explosives that blew out all the trees.

LZ Eagle was the site of our helicopter landing zone, and when we got there, we immediately sat down and compared notes with those who had gone before.

We were told that Puff the Magic Dragon had showed up. This was a C-130 aircraft equipped with huge 7.62mm machine guns capable of firing 5,400 rounds per minute from the air. Although it was a formidable weapon the gooks had managed to hit it and caused considerable damage.

We patrolled the area around Eagle 2, where a hell of a firefight had taken place the previous night, but found nothing to report except for a strange noise that was hard to pinpoint because of the wind that had started to build. After poking around a little more, we finally got ourselves a P.O.W.

We disarmed him where he lay, and then had the medic examine his injuries. Meanwhile, we looked around for more bodies, either injured or dead, as we followed some bloody trails.

When we returned to the firebase, with our P.O.W. in tow, we interrogated him with the help of an interpreter.

"How come they left you?" was the first question we asked him.

Our prisoner insisted that his unit was coming back, and that they had urged him to stay hidden until they returned.

So! It appeared that the gooks were still close enough to come back and hit us again, and then rescue this wounded soldier.

"What size unit?" we asked him.

"Brigade-size," he said, which meant at least several hundred gooks and possibly more.

Since leaving was not an option, we occupied our time filling sandbags and doing all the other things that were customarily done in situations of this kind.

After we'd dug ourselves a bunker, and while I was trying to decide where to sleep that night, a Chinook helicopter flew in, which was big enough to transport jeeps. It dropped off some culvert halves that were used as the top part of a bunker. I spread out about five of them to protect us against the rain and flying shrapnel.

Along about sundown, I put down my bedroll, some distance away from the others and prepared to settle in for the night.

Nighttime was when everything usually happened, and so, we had come to dread the dark. But on this particular night, nothing happened, which I felt was due to the fact that we were well-prepared, and the enemy knew it.

The next day, I went out on ambush patrol with a new guy from our squad named Charlie Wood. Charlie was an ex-LRRP (Long range Reconnaissance Patrol), and we hit it off immediately. After out team had split up, going off in two different directions, Charlie and I sat down to take a break. Everything was deadly quiet.

A short while later, we heard a noise and then Charlie pointed toward two gooks who were standing some distance away, talking to one another. They were carrying M-16 rifles and were dressed in American Army fatigues.

Fighting my first impulse, I got on the radio and reported that we had encountered some gooks in a kill-zone that were carrying M-16s and wearing American military uniforms.

A few seconds later, the orders came: "Kill them!" I asked for a second verification.

The next order adamantly insisted that there were no "friendlies" in the area, that these people were definitely hostile, and that they should immediately be shot.

The next time I looked up, I could no longer see the gooks, but we started firing anyway. The one we managed to hit was mortally wounded and later died. A while later, when we encountered a couple more, they started yelling and waving their American I.D. cards.

Realizing now that they were, in fact, part of a friendly unit, I once again radioed in and explained the situation.

What we had actually encountered was an ARVN unit (Army of the Republic of Vietnam) which consisted of some South Vietnamese soldiers who had teamed up with the Americans. Their battalion commander had decided to sweep through and check out the area. But because he failed to coordinate his activities with our battalion commander, we had no way of knowing that he would be there, which was what caused us to react aggressively.

The battle that subsequently ensued left them with about 150 men, and our side with 17. We were sure they intended to kill us all because of our initial assault upon them.

After it was over, I added this incident to my ever-expanding list of "close calls", and found myself wondering, once again, how I had managed to survive.

We were known as a QRF (Quick Reaction Force), which had no permanent assignment. We filled in wherever we were needed, in whatever area had been hardest hit. We did this at night, after patrolling the firebase and setting up ambushes during the day. Nobody ever had any time off in NAM.

We used an M-79 grenade launcher, also called a blooper or a thumper, which looked like a huge sawed-off-shotgun. Whenever it fired, it did so without a flash, which made it possible to shoot it straight up in the air without causing any problems.

Since it was monsoon season, and our team was being used as a QRF, we were stuck on the firebase for the next few days. We all felt this was a lot more dangerous than being out in the bush, simply because "Charlie" knew exactly where you were. He had the advantage of choosing his time for the attack.

Since we were so vulnerable to night-time attacks, we had placed an M-79 grenade launcher on every bunker around the firebase to fire like mortar tubes, in hopes of discouraging any ground attacks. We decided this was the best defense we had against "sappers" coming through our wire. Every soldier had orders to fire at will all night long while on guard duty, and while this was one way of keeping the enemy at bay, it also made it impossible to sleep. After every round, we would wait and listen intently for a scream or a noise, anything at all that would tell us a round had found its mark.

My old unit, NO DEROS DELTA, was guarding the north side of the firebase while we guarded the south. Wandering over to the north side, I ran into an old buddy of mine, the only other Okie left in that unit, who, as it turned out, had access to about a case-and-a-half of beer.

I was pretty well tuned up by the time I wandered on back to the firebase to go to bed.

A couple of my men, noticing how drunk I was, suggested that I stay close to the bunker. I took their advice and slipped inside the tent rather than walking on back to my bedroll.

Along about midnight, all hell broke loose. It started with somebody yelling "Incoming!" and then the first rocket hit the firebase. While they continued to hit us with one-twenty-two rockets, the two men who'd urged me to stay close to the bunker immediately jumped into it. Meanwhile, I stayed where I was, believing that the assault would soon be over. Although a nearby birm offered a little protection, an explosion about twenty or thirty feet away caused some shrapnel to go straight through my poncho, and that helped to sober me up.

As I was crawling along the ground toward the bunker, my leg got tangled in some wire, and a few seconds later, I got hit. Four of my men immediately grabbed me and pulled me inside the bunker.

Looking down, I saw that there was a large hole burned into my pants, but there didn't seem to be any injuries. While I was breathing a huge sigh of relief, the lieutenant called on the radio and asked for a casualty report.

I took a quick head count and then turned in an "all present and accounted for", not bothering to mention the little skirmish that I had just gone through. At this point, we were still in the bunker, wondering if everything was really over.

A while later, when we climbed out and started popping flares, we discovered that two of our men were dead, and three others from the other squad were injured. They had taken a direct hit.

After loading them onto MediVac choppers, we tried to settle down and get some sleep, but this was always hard to do on the heels of any fatalities.

Eventually the sun came up and I found myself thinking of all the other people who were seeing this sight along with myself. I thought about the personal perspectives that made everyone's sunrise a little different—or even a lot. Sunrise on a battlefield ... sunrise in a jungle... and sunrise back in the states where people looked out on gardens or golf courses and talked about another beautiful day.

It was while I was sitting on the bunker, eating a can of C-rations that I looked toward the spot where I'd intended to sleep the night before. I saw that the culvert halves I had laid out had taken a direct hit, and had I been under them, I would have died instantly.

Whenever a "close call" experience would happen—the kind of thing that no one ever seemed to have an answer for, I would find myself thinking long and hard about it, trying to arrive at some higher meaning. On the one hand, it seemed totally pointless to try to make any sense out of something as senseless as war, and yet, there seemed to be a message contained in these situations, where I continued to survive in spite of all the odds.

As so many men in similar circumstances have done, I began to examine my life more closely—wondering what its purpose actually was, and why I was being spared.

There is an undeniable guilt associated with any situation where others are dying all around you. At the time, I had no way of knowing how long and how far I would actually carry that guilt, or what it would finally do to me. I only knew that there was something to be acknowledged here, something about the true meaning of life, and what God might actually have intended for me.

For the moment, I could think no farther than the overwhelming gratitude I felt for the two men who had insisted that I sleep closer to the bunker than I had originally intended. Their names were Jamison and Lassiter, and I owed them my life, and I wanted to talk to them about that, but as usual, there wasn't time.

The next intelligence report we received told us that we were going to be hit by a unit large enough to overrun us, whereupon our battalion commander decided to send a Recon team straight into their path. This meant sending out 17 men to take on a thousand gooks, which didn't make a whole lot of sense.

"What we're looking for here," he said, "is an 'early warning' which we'll have, once you hit them first. After that, we'll know where they're at, and once you come in, we'll be ready for them."

This struck me as the worst idea I'd ever heard of particularly since we were radar-equipped, which made it easy enough to determine an enemy position. But by then, we had learned only too well that logic rarely had anything to do with it. The officers obviously loved situations like this. And so, that night, a group of ten men went out, including myself. The others had suddenly decided that they needed a little R & R. I was carrying an M-60 machine gun and walking point.

Our mission that night was to hit that unit in order to slow them down on their most likely avenue of approach, and then to withdraw to the firebase. The only problem was getting back through the M-79 barrages, and past all of our comrades, armed to the hilt and ready for a fight. If just one shot was fired, chances were that the rest of the Army would immediately follow suit. After that, it would be something like a piranha fish attack on some poor animal that had accidentally ventured into its waters.

In an effort to avoid any chance of encountering "friendly fire", or any other form of artillery, we moved as far away from the M-79 range as we could.

Once we had set up an ambush. I laid out a claymore mine, and while I was doing this, one of our men leaned his rifle with a fixed bayonet, up against a bush. As I was walking back with the controls, I ran into this razor-sharp bayonet and punctured my arm to the bone.

As the Medic examined my wound, which was bleeding profusely, he told me that he hadn't brought any pain-killers along.

"That suits me just fine," I told him. "I need to stay alert."

Although I meant this when I said it, the pain was so excruciating that I found it impossible to sleep that night, and by the next morning. I couldn't lift my arm. There was some talk of MediVacing me to a M.A.S.H.-type unit, but this would have given our position away, so all I could do was tough it out.

To make things worse, we had to suffer through a severe thunderstorm, which left us all wet and miserable.

Whatever we were expecting didn't seem to be happening, which was rather nerve-wracking, as any extended period of silence is known to be. Armed with a machine gun and a .45, I was becoming a little trigger-happy, and when one of my own men stood up, I saw his silhouette, and immediately cocked my gun. Hearing this, he quickly identified himself, and this was the only thing that saved him.

Once the rest of the team had moved out, I stayed on the firebase with my bad arm, and since I had the bunker all to myself, I figured I'd get a good night's sleep. Before going to bed I piled up a few more sandbags, to ward off the effect of the monsoon season.

Sandbags had many uses in the jungle, and were often worn over our boots to keep the mud from sticking, which worked out extremely well.

A trench had been dug around the inside of the bunker, which was supposed to be a fall-back area, but because of all the rain, it ended up being a drainage ditch.

That night, with nothing better to do, I decided to shoot a few rounds with the M-79, which I did, after talking to the guard for awhile, and smoking a couple cigarettes.

Finally, I said, half-jokingly, "Well, I'd better get back. It's almost time for incoming." After jumping the ditch, I came upon an artillery parapet where two soldiers, were stationed with a 105 Howitzer. They were getting ready to shoot some H & I's, another term for Harassment and Interdiction, a preplotted form of artillery fire designed to keep the enemy on edge and possibly catch them off-balance.

Repeating my remark about Incoming, I started back to my bunker and then I heard someone yell, "Incoming!" I dove into the bunker just as the rounds started hitting. The first one struck the artillery parapet.

Standing alone in a huge bunker can be a frightening experience, with liberal doses of paranoia added. As soon as the rockets and mortars stopped, I got out of the bunker and prepared myself as best I could for a ground attack.

As I ran past the artillery bunker, I pointed my flashlight at the place where the two men had been standing, but now they were lying on the ground. The impact and concussion of the round inside the parapet had killed both soldiers instantly. Their faces had no expressions, and their eyes were still open. One had had his legs blown off, and the other was lying on his back still holding a huge artillery shell, as if he were preparing to load it. This grisly sight gave new meaning to the words "Killed instantly". I found myself thinking that life did, in fact, hang by a slender thread, and that it could snap at any moment. The only thing that I could still do was attempt to save myself, or else, I could do nothing, and die. Because death seemed imminent, I decided I would die fighting.

Once we had rounded up our own casualties, we saw to it that they were MediVaced out, and that took care of another night.

By then, I had begun to feel our losses in a deep and extremely personal way. Despite what we had been told about remaining detached, I felt depressed over the loss of such fine young men as our Radio Telephone Operator, a big kid named Cal, who, before the draft, had been selected to play football with the Dallas Cowboys.

Cal was one of those people who was hard to wake up. One night, before I punctured my arm with the bayonet, and while we were sleeping around the bunker, we heard somebody yell "Incoming!" As usual, everyone immediately dove for the bunker, Grabbing Cal, I shook him as I went by, and then headed for the bunker myself.

A little later on, when Incoming had stopped. I looked out and saw Cal still lying where I'd left him, his body jerking and kicking. A few moments later, he lay quiet. He'd been riddled with shrapnel, a round having landed and exploded just four feet from where he lay, and he died before he even had a chance to wake up.

In later years, I found I was always extremely nervous and impatient with people who wouldn't jump right out of bed after I woke them. And, of course, I always experienced an instant flashback of the incident involving Cal.

Another man was MediVaced out after he lost his hand. We later found it by following a swarm of flies that had been attracted to the stench.

The next firebase we set up was LZ Eagle 2. By this time, our lieutenant was gone and a replacement had been sent in. I was sent off on R & R, and when I got back, I saw that we had a new platoon sergeant and a new platoon leader.

Our platoon leader had been a general's aide in Fort Benning, Georgia where the airborne Rangers originated from. From the outset he made it perfectly clear that he was an airborne Ranger and totally in charge. His name was Vic Crowder and he was "Strictly by the book". His ideas were all pretty stupid, and it didn't take long before Mr. Airborne Ranger and I locked horns.

The thing we needed out here was a West Point Officer, but here he was, and there was nothing that could be done about it.

Whenever I listened to his Ranger-type strategy, I would try to keep silent, but usually I found myself saying with strained politeness, "That just won't work, sir."

The first thing he wanted to do was divide us up into three squads. At the time, we had two reinforced squads consisting of ten men each, but Crowder wanted five and six man squads. I patiently explained that several people, including myself, would soon be leaving, and that the men who were left behind would barely fill out two squads.

Whenever we went out into the bush, Crowder would always radio in under the code name "Airborne Ranger", and because he thought of himself as a survivalist, he never carried anything except a rifle, a compass and a map.

One day we noticed some signs that told us we were nearing a bunker complex. Some trees had been cut with cross-cut saws and the stumps had been camouflaged with dirt and grass so that a light observation helicopter wouldn't notice them from the air. The gooks used the trees to build their bunkers with, and then covered the limbs with plastic, dirt and tree branches.

When Lt. Crowder walked up to warn me that there was a bunker complex about fifty meters ahead, I said, "No sir, we're standing in it right now." The look he gave me reflected his disbelief and inner resentment, which I allowed him to wallow in for a few minutes before I walked him over to the bunker and simply pointed it out.

I watched his jaw drop, and then the next thing he said was, "We'd better check it out for gooks."

"No need to, sir" I said. "If they were in there, we'd already be dead since we're standing in the kill zone."

The next stupid question he asked me was, "Why didn't you check this bunker position out earlier? There could've been gooks in there."

My answer: "And if there had been, they wouldn't have passed up an opportunity to kill an American officer, especially an Airborne Ranger."

"But how would they know I was an officer?" he asked.

It was hard not to laugh in his face. "Well, sir, who else do you see out here wearing sunglasses, not carrying a rucksack, and toting an AR-15 instead of an M-16? Not to mention that you're wearing a much better uniform than anyone else."

Crowder was pretty unbelievable and yet he continued to ask his stupid questions, and make his asinine suggestions. One thing he wanted us to do was set up an ambush in these same bunkers and then wait for the gooks to come back.

I wondered if I had heard him right. But he was standing there, waiting for an answer. Finally, I said, "There are at least fifty bunkers out here, sir. Do you have any idea how many gooks it takes to build that many bunkers?"

He responded with a blank stare. "Well, the fires are still warm," he finally said. "They can't be far."

"That's true." I told him. "If they're even gone."

By this time, my sixth sense was working overtime, as it normally did in situations of this kind. Trying to follow the path of Crowder's thinking, I decided that he might have been looking at this as his mission, if he were to give the order for us to stay in that place and set up an ambush in Charlie's backyard.

In the course of our conversation, I managed to give him a clear definition of a Recon team, emphasizing the fact that the element of surprise always helped, although in this case, that element had definitely been compromised.

Soon after that, we went out on what was supposed to be my mission before R & R. We were told that a Colonel's helicopter had been shot down, and that a LRRP team was missing in this same area.

Our job was to find the LRRP team, the downed helicopter, and the officer, which, was a mighty big job for handful of people. Quite frankly, it was a ridiculous assignment. We knew we were no match for anything that could bring down a helicopter, capture a colonel, and take out an entire LRRP team, but no one seemed to have given this any thought.

Assuming we were being watched, we walked out of the firebase as if we were merely on patrol. Moving south, we eventually circled around and ended up in a place called Hobo Woods, which was equivalent, in its way, to east L.A. It was not a place you wanted to hang out in for a very long time.

When we ran into another bunker complex, Lt. Crowder suggested we set ourselves up there. This, of course, was another bad idea, since the gooks knew the layout of the place a lot better than we did.

Stupid situations. Stupid orders. It never seemed to end. The only end that any of us could ever really imagine was the one that would finally take us out of the game for good.

Thoughts of death, accompanied by sightings of a vision that came to be known as the Death Angel, were not at all uncommon. The first time I saw this apparition—a tall, dark form silhouetted against the sun, I thought I was losing my mind. Then I decided that I *wasn't* losing it, that it had come to tell me something, something I hadn't wanted to know.

You won't get out of this alive! Was the message I kept hearing. It didn't help to know that others were hearing it too, and that they had also seen this ominous Angel of Death.

When I started seeing it in my dreams, it generally wore an NVA uniform, similar to black pajamas. Sometimes I would kill it, and sometimes it would kill me. I wasn't always sorry when it killed me, particularly on those days when I felt that all we were doing was engaging in a deadly game of chess. We would put our wounded in a chopper and send them out, and then some new pieces would be sent in to play, and another game would begin.

Death is the healing that life did not provide, I thought. It is the only thing that can take me out of this, the only thing that can ever make me whole again. It appeared obvious that as I approached the end of my physical life, I was becoming more open to spiritual matters. Still, I had an odd way of showing it. I drank more, partied harder, and, at the same time I thought about God. In the midst of all this, I could only wonder what God was thinking about me.

I was still running on rage, but I was also deeply depressed. Depression hung like a black cloud over my head, and settled softly around my shoulders. I knew I was a victim of sleep deprivation carried to the extreme, as most of us were. Since everything happened at night, we were afraid to go to sleep. We feared that we might roll over and make a noise, or that we might snore, or cough or even breathe too loud. Each night we would lie down with all of our gear close-at-hand. Close meant close enough to reach out and grab it without making a sound. I would lie rigidly in the dark, memorizing the location of everything I might suddenly need.

Special patrol equipment could consist of quite a wide variety of items. For example, a special airborne group had need of all of the following: a camouflage fatigue uniform, a floppy brimmed hat, jungle boots, insect repellent, signaling panel, pen flare gun, flares, signaling mirror, lensatic compass, triangular bandages, ammunition pouches, compress bandages, ammunition, smoke grenade, fragmentation grenade, pic canteen, canteen cover, water purification tablets, pistol belt, pistol belt harness, snap link, bayonet with scabbard, first aid pouch, rucksack, 12 feet of nylon rope, rappelling gloves, lightweight poncho, and an individual weapon. Being responsible for such an extensive inventory of items, under the worst possible conditions, provided yet another reason for our anger and frustrations.

Stretched out on the ground in that long dark night, trying to remember if this thing or that thing was lying to the left or the right of me, I would wonder how it could all have come down to this. A handful of possessions that had come to represent life or death were all I really owned in the midst of this eerily silent blackness. There could be no darker dark than this, so grim and ever threatening, for everything was out here, poised and ready for attack. Another night of interminable length would slowly pass, and then I would see it, the first faint glimmer of light. At first, I would think I had imagined it, that I was seeing it because I wanted it to be, but then there would be this tiny sliver of light, expanding slowly, ever so slowly, and I would know that I had been spared to see another day.

But the safest times could also be suddenly transformed into the most dangerous of times. A case in point:

One day, we were packing up and getting ready to move out of the area. While we were camouflaging ourselves as best we could, an LOH (Light Observation Helicopter) flew overhead. We were about 100 meters from the firebase when the pilot spotted us. There were some Mexican and Hawaiian guys in our unit who might have looked like gooks from the air, but anyway the copter opened up on us with its mini-gun. We immediately scattered like a flock of frightened birds, and then popped some smoke so they'd know we were friendlies.

When the firing finally stopped, we were shocked to see how close those bullets had come. A few had actually hit some rucksacks, but fortunately, got embedded in the C-rations rather than the ammunition or claymore mines that the men were carrying.

After an incident like that, physical exhaustion would finally overtake me, and then, I could sleep as if I'd been drugged—deeply, dreamlessly as children sleep, without a hint of restlessness or fear. But, all too often, sleep was out of the question, for another patrol, another mission, another firefight was usually waiting. And so, sick, exhausted men would dutifully respond, for as long as they were able to endure.

Only the Death Angel seemed to offer any relief from this, since daytime dozing was not possible, because of the oppressive heat, and the flies. Still, it sometimes seemed to me that the Death Angel had another mission, one I had never given any serious thought to.

I had heard that angels often appeared when a person was in a state of near collapse, catapulting them into contact with the angelic realm in order that they might learn how much they still valued life, and also, to remind them of the need to complete some "unfinished business".

Rather than concerning myself with what this war was all about, perhaps I needed to be asking myself what my *life* was all about.

Not an easy question. Ever. Not for anyone I know.

Chapter 7

Each man assigned to a one-year tour in South Vietnam was entitled to one week's rest and recuperation, (R & R) at government expense, at one of numerous Pacific Rim cities. I woke up one day and realized it was my time for R & R—six days in Hawaii, as it turned out. I'd actually lived long enough to earn myself a mini-vacation.

Since it had been a very long time since I'd taken off my boots, I soon discovered that I had a raging case of Jungle Rot, a fungous infection of the skin. The salt water and sand did its part to heal this, and my wife tried to heal the rest. But whatever we had been hoping for—something on the order of a second honeymoon—fell considerably short of the mark.

In a way I could never have explained, I felt totally used up, and oddly foolish in a situation where I was suddenly expected to just enjoy myself. By now, I was burned out with guilt over behavior that, at least by society's standards, was commonly regarded as wrong. Any little thing at all could set off an emotional tirade. Some of the more obvious indicators that something was seriously wrong included: depression, low self-esteem, headaches, chronic fatigue, and an inner urge I could not really identify, but which was actually a desire for self punishment. And, of course, it was easy enough to punish myself by sparking minor or even major misunderstandings between my wife and myself. This made enjoying my period of R & R a near impossibility, but what right did I have to enjoy myself after all the horrible things I'd done? I didn't speak of those things of course, because my wife was still looking at me as if I was this person she had once known and loved. She did what she could to bring some shred of normalcy back into our lives, and while I should have been grateful for this, I remember thinking how ridiculous it all was. What miracle did she hope to accomplish in a *week* after all these months of unspeakable horror? And yes, it was unspeakable. I knew once this was over that there wouldn't be any-one to talk to. I couldn't think of anyone back home who could pos-sibly understand, or who would even want to hear about any of the things I'd been through.

As the week in Hawaii progressed, I began to feel worse instead of better, primarily because I was stricken with a bout of malaria. During our mission in the Hobo Woods, the medic had run out of malaria pills, and so, it hit me in Hawaii.

I can remember sleeping all the way back to Vietnam, and when I got off the plane, a friend of mine, who was shocked at my appear-ance, immediately arranged to have me Medivaced to the nearest hospital. Because I had suffered so long with this disease, I was sent to Cam Ranh Bay for a 30-day recuperation period. Cam Ranh Bay was regarded as a relatively safe entry point from the States.

After spending thirty days in Cam Ranh Bay, I returned to my unit with three Purple Hearts, and a little less than 60 days left to serve.

It was subsequently decided that I should stay in the rear, where I could occupy my time with piddly little details until my DEROS, the date of my departure.

Since beer cost only ten cents a can, it was easy to stay drunk, and this seemed like the best answer to everything. By now, I felt I'd had my fill of this man's army. It was true what they'd been telling us—that a man could age ten years after one year in Vietnam. I felt a lot older and wiser now, and I knew that life was a serious business. It had value, but war made it seem cheap and expendable.

Besides, what had I really accomplished since coming here? So far, I hadn't gotten myself killed, nor had I gotten anyone *else* killed. That was really the extent of it. And meanwhile, the war raged on.

Having been sent to the rear, I took full advantage of the extra time I had and asked the clerk to type up some paper that would extend my tour of duty another six months. In this way, I could move up my final discharge date by half a year, and once I was out, I would *really* be out, and no way could I ever be recalled.

I hand-delivered my request to division headquarters while I was getting ready for R & R. I wanted to be home for Christmas, but knew I would have to keep quiet about this since there was always the chance that my extension request would be denied.

Although things seldom worked the way I wanted them to, this time they did, and in less than two months, my request was officially approved. I immediately sat down and wrote a letter home, advising everyone that I would be home for the holidays. It looked so good on paper that I decided not to spoil it by telling them the rest—the part about having to come back for another six months.

Because a lot of the other men had been thinking along the same lines, it became suddenly hard to get a plane out of country, but the Army finally came through.

I arrived in California at a civilian airport on December 24, at 0600 hours, where I was determined to catch a Delta Airlines flight to Oklahoma City.

Although I knew this wouldn't be easy, I begged and pleaded with a ticket agent, and finally told him that it was my birthday, and that I needed to get home so that I could celebrate with my family.

The Delta agent asked to see some I.D., which would prove my date of birth, and once he realized I was telling him the truth, he picked up the phone and started pushing some buttons, and as quickly as that, it was done.

"Because it's your birthday," he said, " and because you're a G.I. coming back from Vietnam, I've got you on a flight that leaves for Oklahoma City in three hours. And, oh yes, you'll be flying first class."

Whatever I said in response sounded awkward and more than a little inadequate, but I was suddenly at a complete loss for words, and entirely too emotional to express what I truly felt.

Once I was seated on the plane a black gentleman sitting next to me introduced himself and asked a few questions about Vietnam. He had been hearing things and wondered if it was really that bad over there. My response was quick and to the point, and after that, he offered to buy me a drink.

I was extremely grateful for the courtesy and kindness that others were showing, since I'd been hearing about the anti-war demonstrations and had already geared myself up to take out the first Hippie that looked at me cross-eyed.

As we approached our destination, I looked out the window at familiar landmarks, and thought about the conversations I'd had with a fellow Okie in Vietnam about flying into Oklahoma City at night. It gave me a terrible feeling to know that he had never had a chance to see this sight as I was seeing it, since they had sent him home in a body bag.

When the plane touched down, I was one of the first passengers out of the plane. I was amazed to see a crowd of people there. It looked as if the entire town had turned out to greet me.

Once we had said all it was possible to say at a crowded airport, we headed on back to the house.

With all of the other cars following ours, we must have looked like a convoy, or even a funeral procession.

While my wife seemed happy just to have me there, my mother was annoyingly inquisitive. She kept asking about my next duty station—where it would be, and what I thought I would be doing.

I avoided answering her for as long as I could, and then finally admitted that I would be going back to Vietnam, but that it would-n't be so bad because I had a rear job. This did put a bit of a damper on things

While holiday leave had its share of happy memories, there were also a number of experiences that would gnaw at me later. A major question in my mind was whether or not I was still suited for civi-lized society. Decent, God-fearing people, the kind who lived in my hometown, would have been horrified to know the things I had done, and there was always the chance that they might find out. I often felt that my skin was transparent, that every ugly feeling and thought that I had ever harbored could be detected by anyone with an exceptionally perceptive eye.

I did not much care for the idea of being scrutinized by such people. I had no desire to endure their criticisms and open disap-proval. It often seemed to me that it would be far better to return to the jungle, where we lived according to a different code, and where we could all take pride in our abominable behavior, and be admired, and praised—and *understood.*

Understanding came at a premium these days. Here at home, it rarely existed at all, and what little I saw of it was rather difficult to define. People did their best but their smiles were stiff, and they often seemed uncomfortable around me. Then again, it might have been my discomfort that they were sensing, and reflecting back to me.

It suddenly occurred to me that hanging around home too long could actually be hazardous to one's health. I was thinking of what had happened to my buddy, Phil LaCrosse, who had stayed home longer than he was supposed to because his wife was about to have a baby. They lived in St. Louis, Missouri, and after the baby was born, he took his punishment and reported in.

Phil was a Pvt. E2 when he came to our company. He was a damned fine soldier and an ideal candidate for sniper school, which was the reason I recommended him. One day, he showed me a whole lot of pictures of different girls that he was carrying around in his wallet. When I commented on one of them, he said he would have her write to me. Shortly after that, Phil received a 'Dear John' letter.

After taking his training, Phil came back to the unit with his new sniper rifle, eager for his first kill. It was obvious that he wanted to take out his anger on the war and, in the process, he fell for one of the oldest tricks in the book.

I had taught him to walk point, and one day, while he was doing this, a gook suddenly jumped out in front of him, and then started running down the trail. Phil took off in hot pursuit, hoping to get in a good clean shot. He ran into a command detonated mine, and although he was a big, strapping guy, he was no match for this kind of warfare. While he lay there screaming for help, two men tried to get to him, and were badly wounded. As his agonizing screams continued, a couple gooks started shooting, and then, when he quit screaming, they shot him again. This continued for more than an hour before he finally died.

I wasn't there that day but I heard about it, and it made me think of a song written by Johnny Horton called "Johnny Reb". In one verse, he talks about seeing "the young boys as they began to fall. You had tears in your eyes 'cause you couldn't help at all."

I had very nearly convinced myself that I didn't want to be part of any more of this kind of brutality—that I didn't want to see or hear about it ever again. But then, while I was home, I got to thinking about what small-town life was like and what few career choices I would have. I could go to work in a local furniture factory or take up farming.

I decided I really loved the Army, and wanted to re-enlist for another six years. My decision was influenced, at least partially, by a desire to assert my own manhood in matters of this kind rather than allowing myself to be swayed by the women in my family.

Once I had fully stated my intentions on paper, I mailed off what I had written, and soon afterwards, I received a 'Dear John' letter. After discussing it with the chaplain, I was told that this was what I should have expected, since it was only par for the course. Even so, the chaplain said he would see what he could do as far as arranging another R & R.

I had been diligently saving my money in an effort to build a little nest egg, and while I was reluctant to spend any of it, I now made another trip to Hawaii in an effort to save my marriage.

I listened as my wife described me as a person she didn't really know anymore. According to her, I had taken on a whole new circle of friends, and my conversation consisted primarily of war stories. She informed me that she had absolutely no intentions of leaving our little hometown and following me around to remote parts of the world.

I was a little disturbed to hear that she felt she no longer knew me, since I seemed to be literally *surrounded* by people who no longer knew me, or even trusted me. Even military people.

An incident I would always remember occurred in an Army supply store where I had gone to get the ribbons for my uniform. While I was there, an officer walked up to me and said, "Sergeant, you're not authorized to buy those ribbons if you haven't earned them."

I stared at this officer in stunned silence for a moment or two before showing him my orders. I can remember that his attitude immediately changed after that, and that he congratulated me for being such a credit to the Army. Meanwhile, some curious onlookers had begun gathering around, making me feel highly conspicuous, almost as if I had done something wrong.

There were certain advantages and disadvantages associated with those commendations. The advantages included the fact that they helped me to get promotions, and later assisted me in getting my VA disability.

A distinct disadvantage existed in the fact that people constantly asked how I had earned my medals, and for as long as I would tell them my war stories, they continued to buy me drinks. After a while, I began to feel like a freak, and I could sense the resentment among my fellow soldiers, especially the young officers. A few of them even took the time to check out my military record to see what I had really done in 'NAM.

But, assuming a more modest attitude toward my exploits during the war didn't seem to work either. On those occasions when I deliberately didn't wear all my ribbons, senior officers would remind me that I needed to set an example.

After a while, when I was asked what I had done to earn my medals, I would simply laugh and say: "I just killed a lot of people." There was something in the way I said it that usually brought a quick end to the conversation.

Although I had hoped, even *expected* that the medals would help me to secure a good job after I returned to civilian life, they actually worked against me. On every job application, where they asked for military information, I would fill in the citations I had been given, and what they were for. This was usually the end of things, rather than the beginning.

One day, another Vietnam vet clued me in on what I was doing wrong. "The more military stuff you put down," he said, "the faster you'll disqualify yourself. They figure you'll lose it somewhere along the line and end up killing everybody around you. The more medals you've got, the crazier they figure you are."

Once I'd completed my extension in 'NAM. I was assigned to a base that had a Recondo school. After signing into the post, I found the unit, and requested an interview with them. I was immediately accepted.

My duties at this Recondo School Duty Station were to train soldiers to do what I had done in Vietnam. We soldiered hard, and partied hard, and since we all thought and acted alike, I figured we were all pretty normal.

It was the right job at the right time, because it helped me through my divorce, which got pretty ugly in the end. After it was over, all I had left was a car and some bills, and a six-year commitment to the Army.

While I was teaching at the Recondo School, I became a little wilder and crazier because of the group I was hanging out with. They were the kind of group you knew you could count on in any situation, but they also liked to make you feel stupid whenever they could. They could quote the field manual, chapter and verse, and had memorized the proper patrolling techniques for a Recon Team and recited it by rote. *Perfection* was the name of the game, and nothing less was acceptable.

We usually spent our weekends in a little bar that opened at noon and didn't close until we closed it. As part of this little clique, I prided myself in drinking up to a case of beer a day, and by the time I got my orders to go to Germany, I was drinking Scotch on the rocks out of a 12-oz., mug.

By this time, I had started experiencing some flashbacks, but I kept referring to them as nightmares. And whenever I became overwhelmed by emotion, crying uncontrollably over my buddies who had died, I blamed it on a hangover.

I had only been in the states for six months when the orders to Germany came through. I managed to circumvent them because of a scheduled appointment with the promotion board, where I was elevated to a staff Sergeant E-6.

The next time the orders came through for Germany, I was on my way to Ranger School, and this too, was accepted as a legitimate excuse. But the excuses eventually ran out and the next time my orders came through, I knew I would have to go.

First, I was given a 30-day leave. I spent it with a woman I had met while in Ranger School and during her visit to Oklahoma she became my wife.

I went on to Germany to set up housekeeping so that my new wife could join me. But by the time she arrived, I had been busted back down to Sergeant E-5, and nothing was going right.

Eventually, I managed to get with some of "my own kind" and after that, I was promoted back to Staff Sergeant E-6, and became a top-notch instructor.

Letters of appreciation began pouring in from Generals and other NCOs, including a Full Bull Colonel who was the one responsible for reinstating me to my previous rank with time in grade and payment of all back monies, which had been calculated retroactively. Apparently, there was a God and He still knew my name!

I volunteered to go to an Airborne Ranger Battalion and was immediately accepted. This group consisted of an elite group of my kind of people. After three years, I finally returned to the states, with my wife, and one child.

After another 30-day leave, I headed to Fort Benning, Georgia where I was called out of the group during the first 24-hours and sent to the leadership Department's Command Sergeant Major. He told me about a job he had personally selected for me. I was to be assigned to the Physical Training and Hand-to-Hand Combat department for the purpose of training officers. This turned out to be a pretty "cushy" job compared to some others I'd had. There was no field duty, and once again, I was working with an elite corps. Then too, my weekends were usually free.

The only problem I had was that I was finding it hard to stay sober. And my flashbacks were getting worse.

At that time, I thought that a flashback was something that a drug addict experienced after an overdose. And so, when my nightmares began occurring during the day, I decided I must be going crazy.

What was actually happening was that my memory was constantly being triggered by sights and sounds that were causing me to make a lot of bad associations. All it took was seeing a guy who looked like a buddy of mine who had died in Vietnam, or maybe a name would be the same, or I would see a soldier wearing the same unit patch as mine. Sometimes it was just snatches of conversation that I happened to overhear—or a song, that would set me off.

By the time I got out of the service, I had a wife, one child and another child on the way. While I was determined to start a new life, I had no idea how to go about this with so many ghosts still dancing around in my head.

Fearing the onset of insanity, I decided I would have to hide my problems in the only way I could. The really important thing, or so it seemed, was to act normal. To keep functioning and to never let anyone know. This meant I could never again take anyone into my confidence. I would need to be my own best friend, and also, my only friend.

I had two children with my second wife, and I also had a major drinking problem. Although I was sure that I could stop drinking whenever I wanted to, I rarely wanted to, and even when I did, my sobriety never lasted more than one or two weeks.

The fact was, I didn't much care for the world when I was sober. I had tried to adjust, to somehow make my way in a civilized society. I had tried to fit back in, and there were times when it seemed to be working, but something would always go wrong.

The worst things happened at night, just as they had in the jungle. At night, in my dreams, my subconscious mind ran wild and free, and there was nothing that I could do about it.

I would dream about being pinned down and playing dead. Night after night I would be lying as still as death on the ground, holding my breath, and that's what I did in my sleep. One night, I held my breath so long that it finally woke me up and jumping to my feet, I sank dizzily to the floor.

My wife had learned to expect anything since the things that happened often involved her. Any sound she made in her sleep—a snore, a cough, anything at all was often enough to startle me awake, and thinking that a gook had somehow managed to sneak up on me, I would instinctively react. Once, I jumped on top of her and nearly strangled her to death.

Another time, when she kicked back the covers because she was hot, this too awoke me with a start, and before I could stop myself, I karate-chopped her and gave her black eye.

Still, I was working hard and taking good care of my family, and I felt that this counted for something. Responsible people didn't deliberately sabotage their lives, so how could I be an alcoholic?

After a while, my wife got tired of trying to explain it to me, and she finally filed for divorce.

Soon after the divorce, I started dating another girl who invited me to come to church with her. I also started going to Alcoholics Anonymous meetings, but didn't notice any great improvement in my life.

And then, one Sunday, I opened the newspaper and saw an ad directed at Vietnam Vets. It asked certain provocative questions that were difficult to ignore. Things like: Are you having problems in your marriage, and on the job? Do you feel you are drinking too much? Are you haunted by bad dreams?

As I read all the questions, I realized that I had every symptom that they were talking about, and for the first time, I realized that *none* of this was normal. I ended up calling the number that had been printed in the ad, and someone on the other end invited me to a meeting. At the meeting, we were all given some forms to fill out, and when I got to the part about military decorations, I reluctantly filled it in.

The people who were there reminded me a lot of myself. They all seemed nervous and impatient and angry, and I knew that a lot of them had pretty much given up on themselves. There was one guy there who had been a 1st Lieutenant in Vietnam, and now, he was emptying trash cans. It was hard to decide how he felt about this since there was no real expression on his face, and his movements were pretty robotic.

I listened as other people talked about their flashbacks, and finally realized what these actually were.

The most profound experience of all happened one night while I was driving along a lonely stretch of highway, reliving the blood bath of April 27th, 1969. I allowed myself to feel a little smug for having come through this one relatively unscathed, although it was true that I had nearly lost my hand. And it was while I was marveling at my own strength and extraordinary combat skills, that a voice suddenly said, "My son, do you really think you were that good?"

The voice, as audible as any sound I had ever heard, literally stopped me in my tracks! I pulled off to the side of the road and got out of the car. I checked the trunk, looking for a tape recorder, or any other kind of transmitting device that might have been responsible for sending this message. But there was only a jack, a few tools, and a spare tire back there.

The hair on the back of my neck was standing straight up and I could feel my spine tingling as the voice continued. "You lived because I let you live!"

What was going on here? It hardly seemed possible that I could toss out a question, and receive and answer this quickly, as if someone had heard me and was actually responding to what I had asked.

Someone. I looked around. And then I tried another question.

"So, what sense does it make? All those close calls, and yes, I remember them all. The bullet between the fingers. That day, when I should have been killed three times in a matter of hours, other people were killed that day, and those guys were my buddies, and they didn't deserve to die, and I don't deserve to live with the guilt I've been carrying ever since. So, where's the sense in any of it?

"The dead are with me in a better place," the voice responded calmly.

"But you took the wrong ones!' I blatantly insisted, to *Someone* or no one at all. "We've got good guys and bad guys here, and it was the good ones you took! It simply wasn't fair.

"Wasn't it? But the good ones don't need a chance to redeem themselves."

By now I was shivering with cold, or something that might have been cold, but somehow I knew that it wasn't.

I had heard about this kind of thing. Disembodied voices, and messages that came with sudden clarity and purpose, that couldn't be dismissed or denied. All right so, now I was hearing such a voice, and whenever I asked it a question, it shot back an answer, and I had the feeling that we could keep this up all night.

We?

Once again, I looked around. But no—the voice seemed to be coming from somewhere inside me—from deep inside my spirit—or my soul.

A religious experience? What was a religious experience? Was it God talking to someone? And if it was, then wasn't it also a religious experience when someone was talking to God? I had done my share of that! There had been times in the jungle, in bunkers, in foxholes, in tight spots or even *impossible* spots when I had talked to God in an effort to settle things between us before the end came. And in the event that I survived through some miracle or other, it seemed only fair to make my covenant with God, and I had done that too.

So, what was happening now? So many of my friends had died, but I was still here. Did I still have a job to do, something connected to whatever I had promised Him at that time?

Back inside my car, I slumped against the seat and breathed a heavy sigh. Sitting out on this deserted strip of highway, it suddenly occurred to me how things would look to a highway patrolman if he happened to cruise by. Only moments before, he would have seen a man sitting behind the wheel of his car, shaking his fist at the heavens and shouting in angry frustration.

"So, what's your story, buddy?" I could imagine him asking.

"Me? Oh, don't worry about me, officer. I'm okay. I'm just having it out with God."

Drunk and disorderly. That would have been any cop's logical assumption at that point, and once he smelled beer on my breath, he'd be certain.

Well, I wasn't drunk, but I was definitely thinking about getting that way. How else could I stop those relentless visits from the Death Angel? He liked to haunt my dreams and bring me, as quickly as he could, to a point where I was cowering in front of him and pleading for my life. But sometimes, I wouldn't *permit* myself to cower; I would try to stare him down as he regarded me with a cold and haughty look.

Even in my dreams, I fought to retain the warlike tendencies I had developed during my tour of duty in Vietnam. Everyone knew that combat veterans had been conditioned to fight, to be courageous, and to never admit defeat. Awake or asleep, it was simply not part of my nature to plead, or give in.

What I hadn't quite counted on was suddenly confronting some other side of my nature, some hidden aspect that had never really bought into any of this, a part that had me pleading with God, going back to my normal way of thinking and being.

Was this what God had been referring to when he said that I needed to redeem myself? In other words, coming home and drinking too much, and terrorizing my wife, and alienating myself from family and friends, and living in a chronic state of depression wasn't the answer after all? Something more was expected? Something more on top of all the things I'd already gone through?

During the war, I'd learned my lessons well. I'd been a hard case to deal with, but now it seemed that I was coming up against an even harder case.

A disembodied voice in the night. Impossible to explain to anyone. And yet, I had heard it. And—that quickly—I knew that something inside of me had definitely changed.

Chapter 8

If I saw it as a punishment for everything that I had done in the war—if this was to be my punishment for the people I'd killed, the people I'd thought about killing, and all of that infernal score-keeping, then the nights made some sense after all. Those horrible nights when I fought against sleep, knowing that sleep would bring its own special horror, and that I would finally awaken with a gasp or a scream. No rest for the wicked! was the message that kept playing in my head. No rest for the wicked! No rest at all. Not in this life, and maybe not even in the next one.

Whatever was gnawing at my brain was like some dreaded form of cancer, the worst kind, the most lethal kind—a cancer of the soul. And I sensed that it was growing! There seemed to be no way to cut it out without cutting myself out literally. A gun to the head, a knife to the chest, or a razor to my wrists. Yes, I had thought about it. In 'Nam I had fought so hard to live so that I could come home and think about dying. Many others had done it too. Eventually, the suicide casualties would outnumber the casualties of war. Ironic. Incredible. And true!

I could think of nothing else to do except to drink myself into a stupor. It wasn't that I liked to drink, or even wanted to drink. But I also didn't want to see the Death Angel, who seemed relentlessly determined to see me. I drank until I passed out. After that, if I had any dreams, I never remembered what they were.

One day I met with a VA counselor and we discussed my excessive drinking. I expected him to tell me that I was an alcoholic. I was prepared to tell him that I didn't care.

"No, not alcoholism in the classic sense," I was surprised to hear him say. "What it actually is, in your case, is a form of self medication. You've been attempting to treat yourself in the only way you know how. The object is to give your conscious mind a rest."

"By becoming unconscious."

"That's right."

I was relieved to hear it. Although I was obviously destroying myself, I had a logical reason for doing it. That seemed to make it better.

With two failed marriages behind me, I entered into a third. It wasn't long before this third wife grew weary of my Vietnam experiences, along with my nightmares, my mood swings, and all the rest.

Realizing that I was the problem in this marriage, and that I seemed incapable of doing anything about it—I decided to remove myself. This time, before it could turn into a divorce, I simply found a line of work that would keep me away from home. I became a truck driver, and took all the long distance hauls I could, since this enabled me to be with the one person on earth I could truly relate to—myself. I felt that I understood myself better than anyone else ever could. Whenever I had flashbacks, I dealt with them myself. I even decided that I was happy. I was earning a good living for my family, and also, staying out of their way. No one knew about my problems, and whenever I got down on myself, I would simply pull my rig to the side of the road and cry my eyes out. No one was ever the wiser.

In the process, I relived every firefight I had ever been involved in where somebody died. I allowed myself to feel guilty about their death, and I also blamed myself for not doing something more— something, *anything* that might have saved their life.

Occasionally, I would drive through a town where an old army buddy had lived. I would remember our conversations, and how he had talked about home. And how he had described this place—this place I was looking at now. It happened once in Atlanta, Georgia, and as quickly as that, I experienced a flashback that took me back to 'Nam. Right back into the thick of it, with the bullets flying, and the smell of death all around me. That night, the Death Angel came and visited me in my dreams.

I found I could not listen to the Star Spangled Banner without bursting into tears. A ballgame on TV, something I'd hoped to enjoy, would nearly destroy me because of the way it began—with the players standing together, with their hands over their hearts, as someone off-camera sang the National Anthem.

So very many people had paid the price for freedom in this land, trading all of their tomorrows for our todays. I found I wanted to 'square my account' with somebody, but I didn't know who—or how to go about it.

It made me sick whenever I saw kids in gangs who thought they could say "No fear!" I was disgusted with dishonest politicians and all the activist groups who had done nothing to help preserve the rights of this country, but who felt they were justified in demanding those rights, and who fed on the milk and honey. Those who died had also died for them, the ones who constantly complained about having their rights violated.

Out on the road I felt free to think whatever I was thinking, and to react according to the way I felt. Anything could be a trigger. A war movie, a certain part of the country, a scary incident, or an angry confrontation with someone who didn't realize that I never fought just to win, but rather to kill, maim, and destroy.

What most people don't understand is that a Vietnam combat Vet was programmed to be a killing machine, and once he is pushed beyond a certain point, his reactions are basically automatic. In war time, a thirty second delay could mean the end of your life, and you tend to remember that, and react to that, long after the danger has passed.

Despite many deep-seated psychological problems, I had no real understanding of PTSD (Post-Traumatic Stress Disorder), and so, I did not realize that this was what I was suffering with. The intensity of the episodes seemed to vary from soldier to soldier, depending on how much training he had, how much combat he had seen, and also, the fierceness of the fighting.

What most people do not realize is that it takes eight soldiers to support one infantry soldier in the front lines, or the jungle. The Recon Team was strictly volunteer, but we did get certain "perks". For one thing, we got ranked a whole lot faster, and we were given priority support, since there were so few of us. We were never ostracized by any of the other men, never referred to as a 'hazard to their health', and the same held true for line units.

As a team, we were an odd conglomeration, a group of guys who had all made an independent choice to be on the front lines rather than learning how to blend into the jungle. Now and again, it would suddenly occur to me that I was literally entrusting my life to people who were virtual strangers to me. I had no idea what any of them were really like, or what they might have done in their lives before coming here. And yet I trusted them in a way that I would never trust anyone or anything again.

In retrospect, it seems strange that I could have come out of the Army and managed to function in a way that somehow passed for normal. My first line of work was in the agricultural field which presented no real problems since there were never many people around. I then went to work in the oilfields, fitting in perfectly with a group of men who, like myself, were constantly living on the edge. I did a lot of "on call" work which often took me away from home. This helped to sustain my marriage to my second wife, who had no problem with my being gone-only with my being home. Once my drunken escapades had managed to take their toll, she packed up the kids and left, and I went back to AA, where I was encouraged to stay away from my drinking buddies, since they were obviously a bad influence.

I did what I could for myself, but I still couldn't face God. The power of God was frightening to me, and I fully expected to be punished, not only for the things I had done in the war, but also, because I was still mad at Him. I knew I owed Him my life, but all I could think about was all of my friends who had died. Whatever I had promised God while in the throes of my foxhole conversion seemed like a whole lot of mindless chatter now. And yet I had said things, and made certain promises, and I expected to be held accountable.

Throughout that time, I went to church, but I also changed churches several times. I think I was probably looking for one that didn't place so much emphasis on certain scriptures like: "He who lives by the sword shall die by the sword." The only problem was, those that were moving away from the scriptures didn't seem to have much of anything to say. At least nothing I could put my finger on. I guess I wanted something to put my finger on, without having God put His finger on me.

I was still some distance away from "unconditional surrender", but I was beginning to consider it as an option.

I returned to the oilfields to make some quick money in an effort to get out of debt. This time I was working in a different division, and because I was working so hard, the company decided to send me to school for additional training.

It was while I was going to school that I met a fine Christian woman who eventually became my third wife. Because she had children of her own, our combined family consisted of five youngsters, and there were many challenges to be faced. By now, I had learned to suppress my feelings about Vietnam, and although I smoked, I no longer drank.

On Sundays, we would take our five children to church, and people seemed surprised when they saw us together. No one thought it would last, but it did, and little by little, life began to get better.

It wasn't until I went home for my 30 year class reunion that an episode of PTSD suddenly knocked me to my knees. One of my best friends and I made contact, along with some others from the graduating class who had been in The 'Nam. We looked at each other, and in that instant, we all knew that we knew that we knew. As quickly as that, the overwhelming pain and sorrow returned, and the wound was fully reopened.

Not knowing how I would ever get through this, I finally told my wife about some of my wartime experiences. It made her uncomfortable, and I could see that she didn't want to hear any more, but I had to get it out.

Sanity, such as it was, seemed to be hanging on a slender thread as I called an old friend and confessed what I was going through. He urged me to go to the VA for counseling.

In a truck stop where I stopped for fuel, I picked up some tapes about Vietnam. Hollywood's version of The 'Nam had disturbed me greatly, and I suspected that these tapes would do the same. As it turned out, they were actually a Godsend, an authentic account of what that war had been about, and also, what PTSD was all about.

My buddy and I had already discussed PTSD and he knew that I had it, and that I was in urgent need of help. By then I knew it too because my traumatic episodes had begun raging out of control, and it was getting harder and harder to hold myself together.

The VA hospital gave me some forms to fill out—seven long pages of questions that were intended to clarify my reasons for believing that I had PTSD. They asked me what I had seen and done in Vietnam and that, in itself, took ten pages of writing—simply to explain a single firefight. At the end, I decided to ask them a question. I remember scribbling in: "Will this be enough, or do you want more?"

Another block of questions related to awards and decorations. By the time I had listed them all, I figured I had said enough to get their attention, and a few weeks later, I was instructed to report to the VA so that a PTSD board could decide what needed to be done.

I reported in, almost as if I was going to a court-martial. I expected a panel of medical experts to hear my case, and then vote on whether they thought I was lying or telling the truth.

Instead, I found myself in a room with only one person—a psychologist-type, who seemed impressed with my military knowledge and the way I conducted myself during this initial interview.

Having reviewed the forms I'd filled out, he asked me about my nightmares and then told me to describe another firefight in which I had been personally involved in Vietnam.

Although this was a highly unpleasant subject, I found I was at ease with him, and so, I went on to describe the worst battle of all, the one that had happened on April 27th. Halfway through my story, he said he had heard enough to substantiate the fact that I had PTSD.

"Well, you're going to hear the rest of it," I said insistently. "You asked for it, and now you're going to hear it."

After that, I told him about the Death Angel, and as I did, I got the distinct impression that he had heard about him before. Although he wasn't about to acknowledge the existence of such a strange phenomenon, he asked me to describe this vision, and I did. After that, he asked me a few more questions and then closed out the interview by saying he would submit his report and that I would be hearing from the VA in about six weeks.

While I was there, I was taken to X-ray so that they could look at my war wounds. I wondered about this since I had long since resigned myself to the fact that my left hand didn't work as good as my right, that I had torn cartilage in my left shoulder and left knee, and that I suffered with chronic back pain. So what if I couldn't raise my left hand over my head? Everybody had something!

I was soon made to understand that what I had wasn't necessarily acceptable, and that it certainly wasn't inconsequential.

Six weeks later, I was awarded 70% disability from the VA and referred to a psychologist who started working with me on a regular basis. She was a fine person, and a competent doctor, so why did I stop seeing her? I suppose I felt guilty about depriving other people of her time. And anyway, I was tired of rehashing my firefight experiences. Tired, and frustrated, and depressed.

And anyway, I was back in control. I was "dealing with it" by going to work everyday, and earning a living, and acting normal, and trying to put it all behind me.

I still had a problem with God, but then, He probably had His share of problems with me. I felt that He had somehow deserted us 'out there', so how could we be blamed for resorting to survival skills and logic? Maybe logic wasn't quite the right word, but once you were in the thick of it, logic took on a new meaning.

Many years ago, a writer by the name of Philip Wylie had written a book called *Generation of Vipers*. In it, he included a definition of war. "War represents an unreasoned and inarticulate attempt of a species to solve its frustrations by exploding," While this was certainly true, wars had continued to go on, and soldiers continued to fight. And somewhere along the way, they were trained to think in a new way, and it was the right way if they lived, and the wrong way if they died.

The fact that my definition of logic did not coincide with anyone else's had little, if anything, to do with the way that other people felt. The fact was, I could not really identify or connect with anyone around me, so it became necessary to *pretend* I was identifying and connecting, that I was actually relating to people, and that they were relating to me, when I knew in my heart that this wasn't really true.

A major part of the problem existed in the fact that I had been yanked out of Vietnam as abruptly as I had been thrown in.

Coming home to a place that was safe and clean, where I knew people who cared about me, people who stood ready to welcome me home, I felt that I had landed on an alien planet.

The trip had taken thirty hours. Suddenly, the heat, the danger, the agony and death of the jungle were replaced by people in fashionable clothing running around an airport, talking about frivolous things. Their conversation sounded idiotic to me—their concerns so utterly absurd and trivial.

As I thought of all the men who were still in 'Nam, still fighting for their lives, still suffering and dying, even as I stood there listening to the gibberish that was going on around me, I felt I might actually go mad. It seemed to me that I could easily go mad if I wasn't very, very careful—if I didn't work very hard at not going mad, and concentrate instead on remaining sane.

That was where the pantomime, the pretense officially began. I had to pretend to be sane, and happy, and glad to be where I was, and enjoying it all. I managed a few rigid smiles, some words I would never remember afterwards, something that sounded like idle chatter in this airport, and in this world of idle chatter and people smiled back and said things that gave me the idea that I was probably acting all right and getting by with what I was doing.

As time went on, I found I could not stop acting. I couldn't afford to have anyone see the tormented savage that really lived inside of me. I couldn't let them know about the rage and the depression, because then no one would like me, or hire me, or marry me, or even care about me.

I tried to talk to God about all this, but He didn't seem to be saying much these days. I figured He was probably mad at me for being mad at Him, and that He'd decided to send me back out on my own.

On Sundays I went to church and sat there and listened to the service, and tried to relate or connect, but I knew what I was really doing because, by then, I'd become an expert at it.

I can live with this! I thought. It'll be easy to play the game, and get by, and act normal rather than being normal, and who the devil would care anyway, as long as I didn't cause any trouble.

I had no intention of causing any trouble. The trouble was all inside me, and I was determined to keep it there, where it belonged. I was lucky because no one knew that I'd been injured: my scars didn't show.

It made me feel good whenever anyone referred to me as a wild and crazy guy. That seemed only a step away from happy-go-lucky and fun to be with, and that was what I wanted so much to be.

What I really wanted was to somehow get reborn, to start over, to take another shot at this business of living and see if, this time, I could get it right.

But, then in my darker moods, I would find myself suddenly thinking another way—for it was then that I wanted to get unborn, to go to a place of *never having been,* where I could hide away forever, and know that I was safe.

Had my life been a mistake? There often seemed to be no point to it. I had married women who later divorced me. I had killed a lot of people, and I'd drunk myself senseless, and gotten into fights, and spread misery wherever I went. And now God was mad at me, and even though that bothered me, I tried to tell myself it didn't really matter much, because I was used to being alone.

I was definitely alone when I would suddenly find myself sitting with a pistol in my lap, toying with the idea of killing myself.

And I was absolutely alone when I prowled around the house all night, when the thought of going to sleep gave me the same heavy feeling of dread that came with knowing that it was my night to go out on patrol.

And I was alone because no one knew that any of this was going on. One look around a room where people were sitting and talking and laughing, was proof enough. Sometimes it was hard to enter into conversations because I'd lost track of what they were even about. Small-talk. What was it? Certainly nothing about the demons that were living in my head, or this kind of hyper-alertness that I'd developed to get me out of the house before my rage overwhelmed me and caused me to strike out. Looking at these people, it amazed me to realize that they weren't even afraid of me. But I was afraid of me! Feelings of resentment, frustration, helplessness, rage and depression constantly coursed through my veins. Sometimes they got all mixed up so that I didn't really know what I was feeling, still, the force of the emotion itself was overwhelming, and would scare me out of my wits.

I thought about what I had been taught about the enemy, and about the psychological tactics that had helped to convince me that these people were less than human, that they were merely gooks, dinks and zipperheads. They were soulless heathens—godless creatures who deserved to be maimed and destroyed. Could I have done it if I hadn't truly believed that they were a menace to the world and that I was the "good guy" in all this? Was that why God was mad at me? Because He thought I still believed this? And what if I really did?

Examining my feelings about killing, I suddenly found myself immersed in another ocean of conflict. If I didn't still believe it, then I was a murderer—pure and simple. And if I did believe it, then I didn't need God, because it would mean that I'd been playing that role myself, deciding who was worthy and who was unworthy, who deserved to live and who should die.

Maybe that's what God was mad about. He couldn't really like the idea of somebody like me trying to do His job. But I was only following orders. No, that sounded too much like the Germans. By the end of World War II, Americans had learned to scoff at that, and had shown open contempt for the 'butchers' who had annihilated millions of people and then tried to hide behind that evil rationale.

So, all right—there was no real justification for what I had done. Not now. Not tomorrow. Not even while it was happening. War could not be justified, but now and again, it was bound to happen anyway. And people would die, and afterwards, all the same questions would be asked. Why did the questions come afterwards, and not before? It could so easily begin with what Philip Wylie had said. A simple examination of that statement. How in the world could we possibly hope to solve our frustrations by exploding? A wise man, Wylie, in the aftermath of World War II, trying to make some sense of things. But he hadn't, and nobody else ever did either—and so, there was Vietnam.

Chapter 9

Despite my most determined efforts to avoid it, I had no alternative, it seemed, but to keep coming back to my covenant with God. I continued to be haunted by it in ways I couldn't explain. Whether or not God was mad at me was no longer the issue. The fact was, I had always prided myself in being a person who lived by his word. If I said I would do it—I did.

In Vietnam, I had learned to be disciplined, responsible and committed. And even if I had developed and utilized these qualities in the worst possible way, I had done so in the name of democracy and freedom.

But somewhere along the line, I had committed myself to something higher. That had been my covenant with God. God had done His part in allowing me to live, but there had to be a *reason* for my survival. Did I really not know what it was, or was I merely sidestepping the things I had been taught—discipline, responsibility and commitment—which I had so willingly demonstrated in war?

The medals I had been given were presumed to be tangible indicators of courage, and yet courage was a word I was extremely uncomfortable with these days. There was something I hadn't yet done, something I might not even be capable of doing, and yet I constantly heard its call.

Our children had gone off on their own by now and my wife and I were doing more work in our church. We attended a meeting in Los Angeles where we met two people who had been to Vietnam on a prayer walk, and they related an incredible story.

While they were there, they learned that the Buddhist priests had placed a curse on the American soldiers in that land, and these

Christians had rebuked that curse and prayed for healing of the soldiers who survived, who might be afflicted with this curse.

A certain thought entered my mind at that moment which I was too shy to express, and so, my wife expressed it for me.

"Maybe one of you could pray for my husband," she said.

As soon as she said it, I became uncomfortable with the whole idea, not wanting to confess what I had done in Vietnam. Although I later tried to talk her out of going ahead with this, my wife was persistent.

On the day of the seminar, we walked toward the front of the room, prior to the meeting, where a man stood ready to pray for me. By now, I was not at all certain that I wanted this, but before I could say anything, or move away, he came forward and said, " Did you want to see me?"

Because he seemed extremely kind, and totally non-threatening, I told him that I too had been to Vietnam, and that I was having a lot of personal problems.

I was extremely relieved when he didn't ask me what they were. "Say no more," was his only response. "Just stay in this area, and I will pray for you."

I was suddenly overwhelmed with emotion, and bit down hard on my lip, so hard, in fact, that it actually bled. Even so, I could not contain the tears. And then I felt his hands on my shoulders, and there was a warmth in those hands that made my entire body tingle. Suddenly I felt as though a huge weight had been lifted from my shoulders. I saw a quick vision of the Death Angel as it passed before my eyes, and then, it was gone. I had a sense of finality about this experience, almost as if I were seeing the Death Angel for the last time, but, of course, I did not really trust this feeling. Still, I have not seen him since, and through some miracle, he no longer haunts my dreams.

After we returned home from our trip to Los Angeles, I began to feel that I might be ready to visit The Wall. The Wall was, of course, the monument erected in Washington, D.C. commemorating the casualties in Vietnam. Sometime earlier, my wife had given me a picture of it to hang in my den.

As my desire to see The Wall gradually became an obsession, a strange thing happened. One day, my boss called me into his office and told me that he needed to have me take care of some business for him in Washington, D.C.

A free trip to Washington, D.C.—to see The Wall!

As I prepared for the trip, I gave little thought to whether or not I was really ready for this. I had to be! So many others had already faced this mammoth reminder of loss and suffering, and now, it was finally my turn.

Soon after completing the business end of my trip, I drove on to Constitution Gardens, where the Vietnam Memorial stands. The photo in my den had not prepared me for what I actually saw.

The Vietnam Veteran sponsors had asked that the memorial have a prominent site, and envisioned a large park-like area. They therefore requested the western end of the Constitution Gardens. At the outset, they established four major criteria for the design: It had to be reflective and contemplative in character; it had to harmonize with its surroundings; it had to contain the names of all who died or remained missing, and finally, it could make no political statement about the war.

Maya Lin, the designer, chose black granite for the walls. Its mirror-like surface reflects the images of the surrounding trees, lawns, and monuments. The walls point to the Washington Monument and the Lincoln Memorial, thus bringing the War into the historical context of our country.

Each of the walls is 246 feet, 8 inches long. They meet at an angle of 125.12 degrees and point exactly to the northeast corners of the Washington Monument and the Lincoln Memorial. The walls are supported by 140 concrete pilings driven approximately 35 feet to bedrock. At their vertex, the walls are 10.15 feet in height. The stone for the walls, safety curbs and walkways is black granite that was quarried in Banglore, India. All cutting and fabrication was done in Barre, Vermont. The variations in color and texture are the result of different finishing techniques. The names and inscriptions were grit-bed in Memphis Tennessee, using stencils produced through a photographic process. The names were arranged in the chronological order of the date of casualty, showing the war as a series of individual sacrifices and giving each name a special place in history. The names were typeset in Atlanta, Georgia from a computer tape of the official Vietnam casualty list. There were a total of 58,196 names as of November 1994.

It was such an awesome sight that, for a moment, I could not even move. I simply stood and stared at it, not yet ready to approach The Wall, as others were doing, to look for familiar names.

The names would be there, I knew, and when I found them, we would have our sad reunion—nothing at all like the ones we had often talked about.

Twice, on the way to this place, I had had to stop the car and fight to regain my composure. Fight, fight, fight—would the fighting never end? Even here, in a quiet and peaceful place that commemorated the dead, the fighting still went on. I stood and watched as others approached The Wall, running the tips of their fingers over the names of their fallen comrades. I saw them sink to their knees and cry. I saw them cry openly now, as strangers looked on, and family members moved closer, to try and comfort them.

Because I was here alone, I thought long and hard about the need for maintaining control. With tears already streaming down my cheeks, I walked up to The Wall, and looked for the names and yes—they were there. What I hadn't counted on was that the men would also be there, that their voices would play in my head, and that I would see them and hear them again—laughing, shouting, cursing, and screaming out in pain.

That quickly, Constitution Gardens was gone, and the jungle was back. The heat, the stench, the darkness, the sweat pouring down my back, the sweat of fear and the feel of something close—something breathing out there, ready to pounce and kill if I didn't do it first. But where? A dream? Yeah, it might be a dream, sometimes it was, but usually it wasn't and I could smell them out there, and I knew that they were watching me.

I closed my eyes, feeling the pressure inside my head, and the dizziness that left me weak and nauseous. When I reopened my eyes. The Wall was back and I leaned my head against the cold stone. Cold stone. Stone cold. Stone cold dead in the morning.

There it was again. Another flashback. The sun rising. The darkness lifting, and as the birds began to sing I could see a lot of bodies strewn about—they looked like rag dolls except that these dolls had guns—and knives, and some had their hands raised, frozen stiffly, permanently, in a striking position. Death had been only seconds away. A lucky shot in the night had killed someone who might have killed me—someone standing poised and ready, only inches away.

And then I heard a familiar voice, the voice of someone I'd been worried about, someone I'd lost track of several hours ago, but now he was there, with that crazy shit-ass grin on his face, and we looked at each other and laughed. We'd made it through the night, another inky black night with its weird sounds and eerie silences, and we should have been dead but we weren't.

But then, as I looked at The Wall, really looked at it now, I saw his name, and the laughter stopped, and his voice went still inside my head. And then his face changed—it was suddenly pale and white, and he was lying on the ground, shivering and moaning, and a chopper was on its way, but it wouldn't be in time.

It was the strangest feeling, to know that he was gone, and to sense that he was here. Here, in Constitution Gardens, watching me watching him, or all that was left of him now—a grit-bed name on granite.

And then suddenly his face became all of their faces, and all of their names became one. I had a sense of everything melting together, and I looked at the guy standing next to me, and I knew that his tears were mine, and that what we both felt, what all of us felt, was the pain of the living for the dead. The sense of loss was impossible to describe, but there seemed to be no end to it. A bottomless pit of sorrow and loss, and the pain of wanting to die and also live.

To come through this, and somehow be whole again—was that really possible? I wondered. The man on his knees beside me had stopped crying now. I watched as he took a sheet of white paper and pressed it against The Wall. Taking a pencil, he ran it over the paper in quick, impatient strokes, and I watched the impression of that name as it slowly appeared on the page. Folding the paper, he put it in his shirt pocket, and then patted the place where it was. A place right over his heart, where it rightfully belonged, and where it would remain for as long as this man was alive.

Over a period of two-and-one-half hours, I sought out the names of my comrades—there were seventeen in all—and it was cold and raining by the time I was ready to leave.

It felt good to be crying in the rain. Throughout the day, I had been struggling to hide my emotions, but now it didn't matter anymore. Raindrops or tears—who would really know, or even care?

I thought of stopping somewhere and buying a bottle of Johnny Walker Red, but I knew that would only mean trouble. Instead, I thought about all the suffering and the dying in this world, and why it was even necessary.

Was it necessary?

I thought about Christ on the Cross and wondered why anything more had ever been necessary after that? Unless, of course, I was looking at it in the wrong way. Maybe the message had more to do with God's suffering than my own.

The crucifixion of Christ had to be an agonizing experience for God. To see His children turn away from love, from goodness and truth to embrace the kind of evil that would cause them to kill His son, yes, that had to be hard for God. I often felt that God suffered my imperfections, my shortcomings, mistakes and that His heart was heavy but also steadfast in its Love. He would give me as much time as I needed, but my failings—my failings would continue to cause Him pain.

And so, the crucifixion had been only a small part of what God was willing to endure. His face would always be there—in all of it—in the death of an animal, a flower, or a man. Yes, He was there, and we could cause Him all that pain and even more, and He would continue to abide until the pain of His pain became impossible for us to bear. Then, and only then, would wars finally cease, along with man's inhumanity to man.

If, in fact, all the pain of the world was Christ's cross, then—what?

Somewhere, in the back of that thought there might finally be an answer. And just what was my part in all this?

I had been a soldier. I was a soldier. They said I was strong, and courageous, and *bold*.

These were all worthy attributes, given the right cause.

I had volunteered for every military action in which I was ever involved. I had wanted to feel proud of what we did out there. *Our* fighting men were the best in all the world. We were a team! *Our* team. *Our* unit. *Our* regiment.

Still, God had the strongest battalion.

But He wasn't too proud to walk point.

Through the darkness and the terror of night we would continue along together. He would lead and I would follow. And I would listen to His wise and expert counsel:

"Having started out on the way of life everlasting, having accepted the assignment and received your orders to advance, do not fear the dangers of human forgetfulness and error. Do not be troubled with doubts of failure or by occasional confusion. Do not falter and question your status and standing. For, in every dark hour, at every crossroads in the forward struggle, the Spirit of Truth will always speak, saying: *'This is the way.'*"

The End